HIS SECONDHAND WIFE

BY

CHERYL ST.JOHN

MILLS &
BOON

First published in Great Britain 2009
by Mills & Boon, an imprint of Harlequin (UK) Limited.
Large Print edition 2012
Harlequin (UK) Limited, Eton House,
18-24 Paradise Road, Richmond, Surrey TW9 1SR

© Cheryl Ludwigs 2005

ISBN: 978 0 263 23608 8

Harlequin (UK) policy is to use papers that are natural, renewable and recyclable products and made from wood grown in sustainable forests. The logging and manufacturing process conform to the legal environmental regulations of the country of origin.

Printed and bound in Great Britain
by CPI Antony Rowe, Chippenham, Wiltshire

"You're comin' with me."

Kate blinked and glanced around the dingy room. "I don't even know you. I don't know where you live."

"Spread out by Cooper Creek called Rock Ridge. House and livestock. I mean to take care of you. What more do you need to know?" Noah asked.

What more, indeed? Kate's mind whirled with concern for her desperate circumstances, fear of the future and the shock of her missing husband's death. The thought of her detested job in the laundry combined with her mother's suffocating criticism convinced her. Kate had to get away.

And she might never have another chance.

Kate turned, grabbed a gunnysack and stuffed her meager belongings into it. She didn't pause to see if she'd forgotten anything, neither did she stop to think or reconsider.

Maybe she was crazy for leaving with a man she'd never met before. Maybe listening to his promises was rash.

But, then again, this could be the best thing that had ever happened.

Cheryl St.John remembers writing and illustrating her own books as a child. She received her first rejection at age fourteen, and at fifteen wrote her first romance. A married mother of four, and a grandmother several times over, Cheryl enjoys her family. In her 'spare' time, she corresponds with dozens of writer friends, from Canada to Texas, and treasures their letters.

Recent novels by the same author:

SWEET ANNIE
JOE'S WIFE
THE DOCTOR'S WIFE
SAINT OR SINNER
THE MISTAKEN WIDOW
THE TENDERFOOT BRIDE
ALMOST A BRIDE
   (in *Wed Under Western Skies*)
PRAIRIE WIFE
CHRISTMAS DAY FAMILY
   (in *A Western Winter Wonderland*)

The story is dedicated in loving memory
to my sister-in-law, Judy Smith,
who loved to read Harlequin and Silhouette
novels and enjoyed so many of
the talented category authors.

I miss your phone calls, the cheese balls
and especially—your laugh. See you soon.

Prologue

Copper Creek, Colorado
April 1890

A sick feeling dipped in Noah Cutter's stomach as he studied the approaching rider. He dropped the wire cutters and rolled his sleeves down over his arms, snatched the hat he'd hung on a nearby fence post and pulled the brim down to shade his face.

His brother was the only person who ever came to Rock Ridge unannounced, and though Noah hadn't seen him for months, the man on the horse was definitely not Levi.

The horse slowed. Noah raised a palm. "That's far enough."

"I have a telegram for ya!" the rider called in the breathless voice of a young man.

"Stick it on the fence there and ride off."

"The sheriff said it was important you read this. You might wanna send a reply."

"Leave it on the fence then and back off."

The youth slid uneasily from the horse's back and loped to the fence. The breeze whipped the paper for an instant, but he flattened it, found an exposed end of wire and poked the missive over the point. He glanced nervously at Noah.

Noah observed in silence.

The lad grabbed the reins and led the animal a considerable distance away.

Slowly, Noah covered the expanse to the flapping paper and plucked it from the fence. Unfolding it, he read the telegram addressed to Sheriff McHargue.

Holding body of man in mid to late twenties, fair hair, blue eyes. Gunshot. Pocket watch engraved: "All my love, Adrienne." Saloon patrons claim owner from Copper Creek. Advise.

Matt McHargue had added his own note at the bottom, two lines in black ink.

Maybe you'd better go see the body. Let me know if you want me to tell Estelle.

Noah stared at the words until they blurred and his stomach knotted. The pocket watch didn't mean anything to him; his brother owned several and some had probably been gifts from any of the number of women he drew so effort-lessly.

The word "gunshot" leaped out with frighten-ing clarity. The description sounded like Levi, but it probably sounded like a hundred other men in the Rockies, as well. Blond hair and blue eyes didn't have to mean the dead man was his brother.

The message didn't sit well, but he wouldn't bet that this couldn't possibly be Levi. It could very well be. Noah had feared something like this for as long as he could remember. Levi's reckless philandering was bound to get him into trouble sooner or later.

As much disdain as his stepmother held for Noah, he couldn't let the sheriff be the one to give Estelle such alarming news. The dead man might not be her son, but if he was, his mother deserved more consideration.

Noah looked up. "Let the sheriff know I'll tell Mrs. Cutter myself," he called. "I'll set out for Masonville at first light tomorrow."

From where he stood, the lad raised a hand. "I'll tell 'im."

He climbed onto the back of his horse, gave Noah another quizzical glance and lit out.

Losing Levi would be like cutting away another piece of himself. An oppressive sense of dread weighed upon his chest as Noah watched the horse's hooves kicking up dust in the distance.

Don't let it be Levi. Please don't let it be Levi.

Chapter One

The rap on the wood was sharp and insistent. Kate Allen Cutter pushed herself up from her narrow cot and slowly crossed the small dimly lit room while smoothing wrinkles from her faded skirt. She'd left her job at the laundry an hour ago to come home and put up her feet. Her mother wasn't due back from her shift for another half an hour.

She opened the door hesitantly.

A hulking mass of a man stood on the step, his shoulders blocking the late-afternoon sun and casting his face into mysterious shadow. Though the day was fair, he wore a Hudson's Bay coat with the collar turned up and carried a rifle as though it was another appendage. He made no move to displace the weathered black hat pulled low over his eyes.

She didn't know him, and she didn't get a good feeling from his presence. A shiver of apprehension snaked up her spine. She was alone here, and he was as intimidating a man as she'd set eyes on. Any number of seedy characters passed through Boulder on a regular basis.

The length of his shaggy dark hair, his full beard and the concealing brim combined with the sun at his back gave her the impression he'd deliberately planned this time and his arrival to catch her off guard. But that was absurd.

Uneasily she found her voice. "Y-yes?"

"Katherine Cutter?" No preliminaries, no polite introduction; he meant business and his imposing manner flustered her.

"Yes," she said again. "Who are you?"

"Noah," he said simply, as though the name should mean something to her.

"Noah?" she repeated dumbly.

"Noah Cutter."

She blinked in confusion.

"Your brother-in-law," he clarified.

Kate's heart did a backward tumble in her chest while her thoughts whirred chaotically. Brother-in-law? It had been five months since she'd seen her husband, and while she remembered Levi mentioning his family, she'd never met any of them. Why would this man seek her out now? Unconsciously she touched her hand to her breast.

"You…you're Levi's brother?"

He nodded.

She stood in his massive shadow, squinting upward, but he didn't elaborate. Finally she glanced at the shabby room behind her and asked hesitantly, "Would you like to come in?"

"We need to talk."

She took a step backward. "Come in then."

He lumbered past her and stood beside the wobbly table.

Gathering her shawl around her, Kate stepped toward the window and reached for the shade. She'd been resting with the shade drawn and the room was semidark. She raised it and sunlight spilled across the wooden floor. She hurried toward the stove. "Can I fetch you a cup of coffee?"

"No. I'm not stayin'. I came to talk." She caught the odd sound his "s" made when he spoke the word "staying." Boots striking the bare wood floor, he moved to stand with his back to the window and turned to face her, once again silhouetting himself against the light.

"What do you have to say?" she asked.

"How long since you've seen Levi?"

Humiliating warmth infused her neck and cheeks, and this time she had little attention for his odd-sounding speech. She didn't want to admit that her husband had taken off without a word and left her to fend on her own.

"He's been looking for work."

"For how long?"

It made her nervous that she couldn't see his face. More nervous that he was asking this question. "A few months."

"I have bad news for you."

Blood chugging sporadically through her heart, she nervously smoothed her palms over her skirt. "All right."

"He was killed last week."

Kate worked the abruptly delivered information around in her mind for a moment, not quite grasping the meaning. Levi had been killed? He was dead? Her heart hammered painfully. "Are you sure?"

"I'm sure."

"It couldn't have been someone else?" She'd

prayed every day that Levi would return and take her from this intolerable situation she'd been forced to endure since he disappeared. Now that would never happen! "Someone who looked like him or someone using his name?"

"I went to Masonville for his body, ma'am." This time his deep voice was thick with emotion. "It's Levi."

Kate's blood rushed to her ears and pounded. She pictured Levi the way she remembered him, with sun-bleached hair and laughing eyes the color of a summer sky. The hazy image of him cold and lifeless didn't mesh with her vivid memories. Levi dead?

Stars burst behind her eyelids. The bright nimbus of light around the man flickered and dimmed.

The woman's face was alarmingly pale and her eyelids fluttered. Her distraught hazel eyes grew unfocused and Noah caught her as she slid toward the scarred wooden floor, scooping her up in his arms and laying her on the cot.

He turned and poured water from a pitcher into a chipped enamel basin. Finding a cloth, he wet it and carried it back to where she lay.

He dabbed the cool cloth against the curve of her delicate white cheek, the arch of her fine pale brow and over her smooth forehead. Noah hadn't been this close to a woman since his childhood, and the disturbing feelings the nearness created combined with her sweet feminine scent to make his hand tremble.

Levi's Katherine had honey-blond hair and skin as smooth and fair as cream. It was obvious why Levi had wanted her. His brother'd had an eye for the ladies—and they for him. But to take one as a wife was so out of character that Noah hadn't believed it until he'd gone to the local justice, questioned the man and demanded to see the record himself.

This place where she lived was little more than a shack, one room with the barest of necessities, and her faded dress appeared to have been made for a larger woman. Levi certainly hadn't taken his responsibilities as a husband seriously or he would have provided a more fitting home and proper clothing. But then, his brother never had taken responsibility for anything.

Another narrow cot pressed against the opposite wall, raising the question of who else slept here.

A woodstove kept the meager quarters warm, and Noah considered removing his coat, but chose to keep it and his hat on. No reason for sending her into another swoon if she awoke.

He rewet the cloth and dampened her face and neck once again, then reached for her hand to cool a wrist. Her hand lay on the mound he hadn't noticed until that moment—a considerably rounded belly beneath her loose-fitting dress.

The woman was with child.

Noah stared hard at the protrusion, his eyes reading more of his brother's onerous deeds.

If it was Levi's baby.

He blinked and rubbed his face with a calloused hand. Placed the cool cloth over his own eyes and pressed in an attempt to clear his head.

A sigh arrested his attention and he lowered the cloth to observe the woman.

Her eyelids fluttered and lifted, revealing eyes that seemed too dark for such a pale complexion. She turned toward him, so he stood and pulled out a chair to sit with the window at his back.

With one hand under her belly, she rose to a sitting position and swung her feet to the floor. "I'm sorry. I—I've never done that before."

"That Levi's child you're carryin'?"

Anger flitted across her features. "He is…" Her voice faltered and her expression softened. "He was my husband. Of course, it's his child." She raised a hand to tidy her hair and tuck stray wisps into the thick knot on her neck, then looked back at him. "What happened to him? I mean, how did he die?"

"Shot."

"Shot?" Sincere-looking tears gathered in her eyes. Her delicate lips trembled. "Who shot him?"

"A man."

"Is the man in jail?"

"There'll be a trial."

"What aren't you telling me? I'll find out, you know."

"Might be it's better to let—"

"Don't hold it back. I'll go to the sheriff myself and find out if you don't tell me."

"Fella name of Robinson shot 'im over Pony Creek way."

"Why?"

"Caught Levi with his wife."

It wasn't shock that passed behind those hazel eyes, it was more like hurt…and shame. She didn't have anything to be ashamed of.

"How'd you know about me?" she asked.

Before he could reply, the door opened.

Noah turned to see a reed-thin, stoop-shouldered woman in a worn coat enter the room. Her suspicious gaze shot from Katherine to Noah. "What's he doin' here?"

"This is Levi's brother, Mama."

She hung her coat on a hook inside the door, revealing a thin shawl and faded dress. "And where is that no account brother o' yourn? We haven't seen hide nor hair of 'im since he got my Katy in the family way and lit out."

"Mama," the daughter cautioned.

"No sense mincin' around, is there?" she asked. "You'd think the girl would have more sense than to marry on a whim, but you can't tell her a dad-blamed thing. Always was flighty, that one. Always thinkin' she was better and dreamin' of a big house to live in. Told her a hundred times life deals you the rotten hand you deserve, and you just have to play it the way you see it. There ain't no fairy-tale endings to be had."

Katherine's cheeks blushed scarlet and it was obvious she held herself in check from replying.

"My brother's dead," Noah said bluntly, cutting off the woman's bleak tirade. He'd come to grips with the fact himself the day before and had used the better part of the night and this day to work up a plan and the grit to come see Levi's wife.

The older woman had stopped her harangue midsentence and blinked first at Noah, then at her daughter. Her eyes narrowed. "What happened to 'im?"

"Shot."

"Up to no good, was he?" she said with a knowing shake of her head and a gleam in her eye. "Well, you're better off without him, girlie. He weren't going to be no kind of father nohow, and he woulda made your life miserable if'n he'd a come back into it. Now you can quit moonin' and get your mind right and get on with your job and feedin' that kid for the next fifteen or so years till he breaks your heart."

Katherine's eyes closed against the harsh words and Noah's temperature inched upward another degree, though he didn't think it was due to the coat this time.

"Mama, Levi was Mr. Cutter's brother. We should show him our sympathy."

"Him? What about you? You're the one married the weasel and landed yourself in this mess. What's she supposed to do now?" she asked, snidely addressing Noah. "Woman like her with a babe and no man don't stand a snowball's chance in hell. She'll be on her back down at Ripley's inside a year, mark my words."

"Mama!" Katherine objected.

Noah cut in at the same time. "I came to take her."

Katherine and her mother both turned to him and stared.

His abrupt words hung in the air.

"What did you say?" the younger woman finally asked.

"You're comin' with me."

She blinked and glanced around the dingy

room. "I don't even know you. I don't know where you live."

"Spread out by Copper Creek called Rock Ridge. House and livestock. I mean to take care of you. What more do you need to know?"

What more, indeed? Kate's mind whirled with concern for her desperate circumstances, fear of the future and the shock of her missing husband's death. She struggled to clear her thoughts and to focus on what this man was saying.

She'd worked in that godawful laundry since she was eleven years old. She was twenty-five now, so that was over half of her life. She didn't want her child raised in this mean city environment—neither did she want him left on a back stoop all day while she worked, raised the way she had been. The thought of her detested job combined with her mother's suffocating criticism to convince her. She had to get away. And she might never have another chance.

"I can work for you," she said quickly. "I can do laundry and cook and clean. I can learn to do just about anything—garden or help with the stock."

Her mother stared at her.

"I'm a quick learner," Kate added. "And I'm not sickly. What happened a minute ago, that was the only time. You won't have to molly-coddle me."

"What are you sayin', girl?" Her mother raised a hand and pointed at Noah. "You sellin' yourself off to *this man* now? He just wants free labor."

"I got hands, lady, and I pay 'em well," he corrected in a gruff tone.

The woman squinted in suspicion. "What do you need her for then?"

"Appears she's the one needs me." Noah turned his attention to the daughter. "Coming?"

Kate turned, grabbed a gunny sack and stuffed her meager belongings into it. She didn't pause to see if she'd forgotten anything, neither did she stop to think or to reconsider. She plucked her coat and bonnet from the hook, worked her feet into her boots and walked to the door. "Goodbye, Mama. I'll write."

The big man followed her out, took hold of her elbow and guided her to a horse tied at the post.

"I have a wagon at the livery," he said. "To carry the coffin home."

She tied the limp ribbons of her blue gingham sunbonnet under her chin. "Of course."

"For now, it's the horse."

"I'm fine with that."

He placed one foot in the stirrup and, with a creak of leather, hoisted himself onto the saddle, then reached down to her.

"Katy, you crazy fool girl, don't think you can come back here again after you make a mess o' things one more time!" her mother cawed from behind.

Kate took Noah Cutter's gloved hand, stepped on his boot and pulled herself up behind his massive form. He raised his coat and ordered, "Hold on to my belt."

Kate did as told, first encountering his wide leather holster, then finding the warmth of his flannel shirt against her fingers intimate but comforting. He urged the horse into motion and she hung on.

"Katy!"

She didn't look back. She'd been a dolt to fall for Levi Cutter, his handsome face and winsome ways. She'd made a fool of herself and he'd left her behind like so much used garbage. All her dreams for a better life and her hopes of leaving this place had been dashed. Taking a good hard look inside herself, she questioned if her heart had been broken or if her pride had simply been wounded.

The ache in her chest was more shame than hurt.

Maybe she was crazy for leaving with a man she'd never met before. Maybe listening to his promise of a home and setting out without a backward glance was rash.

But then again, this could be the best thing that had ever happened. Maybe there was still a chance for her and her baby to have a good life.

And she'd be crazy *not* to take a chance on that.

Chapter Two

The bearded giant was silent the entire ride
to the livery, as well as while he prepared the
wagon, tied his horse to the rear and ushered
her up to the seat. The brim of his black felt
hat shaded his face the whole while, so without
deliberately staring, she still hadn't had a good
look at the man.

For several minutes Kate studied the plain
pine box that held her husband before settling
herself and determinedly looking ahead. She
hadn't had time to absorb all that was happening and still felt a little numb. She was sure
reality would catch up with her later.

Finally, Noah Cutter climbed up beside her
and took up the reins in hands sheathed by
tanned leather gloves.

"How far is Copper Creek?" she asked.

"'Bout a day and a half's ride west."

"You mean, we'll be traveling all night?"

"We'll camp to rest the horses."

She nodded and prepared herself for the journey and the new experience. Her stomach felt a little queasy now that she was going through with this. "I've lived my whole life in Boulder."

He didn't respond, so she took her last look at the city she detested, thought of all the miners' and well-to-do residents' clothing she'd washed and ironed over the years, and said a silent good riddance.

Even if she had to do laundry for this man and his family for the rest of her years, it would be less of a burden than scraping out an existence on her own. "Tell me about your home."

"Run several thousand head on the Rockin' C. Good water and grazing."

"What about the house?"

"My father built it. Two stories, a front porch. The hands eat in a separate building."

"Do you have a family there?"

"Levi was my family."

No wife or children? "Where will I stay?"

"Four rooms upstairs, one is mine. You can have one on the opposite end."

"I *will* work for my keep, I was serious about that."

She felt his gaze on her, as though he was sizing her up for her usefulness. She glanced toward him, but he looked away, hair and hat brim once again shading his face.

"Is the Rockin' C where Levi grew up?"

He nodded.

"He never told me much about his family. I never knew where he was from. Does your father know about…about what happened to Levi yet?"

"My father's dead."

"Your mother?" she ventured.

"Mother, too. Wired Levi's mother. She'll be expectin' us."

"You and Levi had different mothers?"

He nodded again.

Kate studied the countryside, weary of pulling information from the taciturn man. There was snow on the mountain peaks, but the conifers blanketing the lower regions were a dozen shades of vivid green. A craggy range blanketed in white caught her attention and she pointed. "Look how much snow is left."

"Indian Peaks," he replied.

They crossed a river at a shallow spot where farther down, it fed into a wide lake. "Oh, it's so pretty. It's turquoise."

He squinted toward the lake she indicated without comment and guided the team up the bank.

Noah followed a rutted trail that cut around rock formations every so often.

"The rocks are so big! You can almost imagine that the shapes are animals or faces, can't you?" Kate studied the enormous jutting stones. "Have you ever seen anything equal to them?"

He glanced at her, then away.

She straightened her skirt primly. "You're thinking I've lived in Boulder all these years and never seen much of anything. It's a shame, isn't it? I always wanted to travel, to see all the sights and the country beyond the city. Levi was going to take me after—well, he was going to take me. Have you traveled many places?"

"Not many."

She'd never traveled farther than the streets

of the city where she was born until yesterday. "Have you been in other states?"

He nodded.

"Where? Have you seen the ocean?"

"I've been to Texas and back. Seen Nebraska and Kansas."

"I'd love to see the ocean. I've read about it and I've seen paintings. I saw an exhibit once. An artist from Maine had a show and gave all the girls at the laundry a ticket to go see her work. Lovely pastel colors they were, blues and greens and lavenders. Pinks, too. It would be ever so lovely to be able to paint like that, don't you think?"

He shrugged as though he'd never thought about it.

The sun dipped low and the air took a chill. Kate pulled on her coat and fell silent.

Eventually, Noah led the wagon toward a stand of cottonwoods that lined a streambed and brought it to a halt.

Kate studied her surroundings. "Is this where we're spending the night?"

With a grunt, he climbed down.

She stood, her muscles stiff from the long

ride on the hard seat, and he came around to help her. She studied the top of his hat, the expanse of shoulders in that coat, and accepted the gloved hand he raised. "Oh, oh my. Oh, dear." Her feet touched the ground and her hips and back complained. "Where shall I—um?"

He jerked a thumb over his shoulder, indicating the shrubs and trees along the stream.

"Oh. Thank you. I'll be right back."

Noah glimpsed her limping toward the stream and unharnessed the team. He'd never known a person could talk so much. Katherine had barely paused for breath since they'd left Boulder. Not that he minded. As long as she didn't expect him to keep up one side of the conversation, she could talk herself hoarse if she chose. And she might, if today had been any indication.

He untied his gray and led all three animals to the stream to drink. Once they'd had their fill, he tethered them where they could crop grass. From his saddlebags, he took a dented coffeepot and fixins for a meal.

The young woman returned and removed her bonnet. "What can I do?"

He gestured to the pot. "Need water."

She picked up the container. "I'll be right back."

He watched her leave. Of course she'd be right back—where else would she go? He found a dry limb, broke it up and, with sticks for kindling, got a fire started.

Kate returned with the pot. "Do you have a tent?"

"No."

"Are we going to sleep out in the open, then? That will be an adventure. Once when I was small, Mama and I didn't have a place to stay for a few weeks and we slept under a broken wagon behind the stables. It didn't rain, but it did get cold at night. I remember looking up and seeing all the stars. I'm sure we'll be able to see even more of the sky out here so far from buildings."

Noah sliced salt pork into the skillet and let it sizzle before prying open a can of beans with his knife.

"Do you do everything with your gloves on? I've never seen anyone do that, but I've never known any cowboys or ranchers up close. Guess it keeps you from cutting yourself on the can, huh?"

By the time the food was done, night had fallen. Noah removed his gloves and divided the food onto two tin plates. He handed one, along with a spoon, to Katherine.

"Thank you." She took a seat on the ground beside the fire.

Out of habit, Noah situated himself so that his hat shaded his face from the glow of the flames.

Kate kept silent long enough to eat. Finished, she picked up the empty skillet. "I'll wash these in the stream."

Noah handed her his empty plate and she got up and moved away.

He laid out a bedroll on either side of the fire, checked the chambers in his .45 and sat on his blankets.

"What shall I do with these?" Katherine had returned.

"Stand 'em against that log. Fire'll dry 'em."

Noah watched her arrange the skillet and plates with great care before settling on the other bedroll and removing her shoes. She unfolded her blanket and lay down, pulling up the wool covering.

Noah settled his hips into a dip on the hard

ground and closed his eyes. Tomorrow he would have to see Estelle and deal with her.

"Did you ever see anything equal to all those stars in the sky?" Katherine asked. "It makes me feel so small lying here. Just think, somewhere in a foreign land, maybe in Spain or Egypt, people like us are looking up and seeing the same heavens at the same time. And they're wondering about us."

"Could be it's daytime there," he replied matter-of-factly.

"Well, somewhere far away it's night," she said, unflustered by his lack of imagination. "Do you know what the constellations are called?"

"Some of 'em."

"What's that one?"

"North Star, part of Big Bear, and over there's Little Bear."

"Imagine," she said on a sigh. "Explorers have been finding their way across oceans guided by the same stars for all of time. All the people who ever lived, people in the Bible even, have seen the same stars."

"Some have probably burned out."

"Maybe."

Didn't she ever wear down? What had he gotten himself into?

"Thank you for coming to tell me about Levi today," she said, her soft voice carrying across the flickering fire. "And thank you for knowing I'd need your help. I wouldn't have wanted my baby to grow up like I did. I want better for him. Levi was going to move us somewhere nice, somewhere so that our baby could go to school and grow up with friends and neighbors around."

Noah suspected that Katherine would never have seen Levi again, even if he hadn't been killed.

"If you hadn't come, I'd have been stuck in that place," she said. "So…well, thanks."

"Get some sleep. We move on early."

A few minutes later her voice once again carried across the fire. "Are there any wild animals out here?"

"Maybe."

"Are we safe?"

"The fire and our scent will hold 'em off."

"Oh."

Finally silence.

* * *

He spent a restless night, thinking of his brother's body in the wagon bed, the woman across the fire and what he was going to do with her and a baby. He'd slept hard for a couple of hours, then woke with a start to check his pocket watch.

After rolling his blankets, he made a trip to the stream, watered the horses and harnessed the team. He rekindled the fire, stirred dough and baked a pan of biscuits.

Katherine woke to the smell and sat, immediately pressing a hand to the small of her back.

He regretted making her spend a night on the ground and two days on a wagon seat, but he would have her safely to his house later today.

She was strangely quiet that morning as she got herself ready. When she sat near the fire, he handed her a plate of biscuits and a cup of coffee. "You all right?"

She nodded. "Thanks."

Without another word, she ate and drained her cup. She then took the skillet, plates and cups to the water and returned with them clean.

"Seat's hard," he said finally. "I can spread blankets in the back."

She seemed to consider, and he imagined she thought of riding beside Levi's coffin before she declined.

Instead he used the blankets to pad the seat before he helped her up.

As the morning wore on, her silence burned off like the dew, and by the time the sun was high and warm, she was chattering beside him as though she'd never stopped. She commented on the shapes of the clouds, the spring green of the leaves and plants, the snow on the peaks in the distance and the degree of warmth from the sun.

Noah was plum tuckered from the effort of keeping up with her constant stream of dialogue. But she didn't seem to care that he rarely replied, and most of her questions were rhetorical, and so it was with supreme relief as they reached Rock Ridge that he decided she wouldn't be difficult to have living under his roof.

His only experience with women in his adult life had been with his stepmother and the wives of nearby ranchers, none of whom had ever inspired him to take one of his own. No woman would ever want him, anyway.

"Are those your cows?" Katherine asked as they passed a herd grazing along a grassy slope.

He nodded.

"I can hardly wait to see my new home." Excitement laced her voice and Noah tried to imagine the Rockin' C through a stranger's eyes. To him it had always been home.

From the top of a grassy ridge, the entire valley where the ranch buildings sprawled came into view. Trees dotted the landscape, a pond glistened in the sunlight and a long, shallow riverbed snaked along low ground.

Nestled between windbreaks of cottonwood and aspen, the house, meal kitchen and other outbuildings were the only flecks of white on the landscape.

"Oh," she breathed in awe, and was silent for several moments.

He couldn't help wondering what she was thinking, but as usual he didn't have to wait long for her thoughts to tumble out. "It's beautiful. The most beautiful place I've ever seen. The best I could have imagined. The house is so big. How many people live in it?"

"Two now."

"What about your hands?"

"Bunkhouse."

"Don't you have other helpers?"

"Marjorie Benson, wife of one o' the hands, comes twice a week to clean and do wash. They have a cabin a mile yonder."

"Who cooks for the hands?"

"Fergie. Bunks with the others."

"So you've been living in that big place all by yourself?"

He nodded.

"What about your stepmother? Levi's mother, where does she live?"

"Fancy house in town."

"Fancier than *this* place?"

Noah led the team closer to the house, and the closer they got, the bigger Katherine's eyes grew.

"Inside needs some fixin' up," he told her. "I reckon you could do that."

Noah stopped the team between the house and the barn. Two men came forward to unhitch the horses. A couple others stood outside the barn, watching with obvious curiosity.

Noah climbed down, then assisted Katherine.

He glanced at the men, straightened and said brusquely, "Levi took a wife. This is Katherine."

The men immediately doffed their hats and nodded politely. "Ma'am."

Uncomfortable with being a spectacle, she merely nodded a greeting.

"Grab a couple sawhorses and bring the coffin in," Noah ordered the men. "To the dining room. Bring somethin' to use to pry open the lid."

One man ducked into the barn. The one closest to the wagon held his hat against his chest. "How do, ma'am? I'm Tipper Benson. That was Lucky."

"Pleasure to meet you, Mr. Benson."

Noah grabbed the sack that contained her few possessions, gestured for her to follow and guided her toward the house. The front porch shaded the entire front and curlicue trim enhanced the beams and the rails. Noah opened the front door and led her into the cool, dim interior.

Kate observed her new surroundings with interest. The enormous rooms held an assortment of upholstered chairs and oak tables. She noticed a stone fireplace with a plain wood mantel and rugs on the wood floors. Noah pointed to the stairway, so she gripped the railing and preceded him. An empty plant stand stood on the landing next to a window with a view of the side yard. They reached the top and faced a long hallway with doors on either side.

"That's mine." Noah pointed to the first on the left, but kept moving.

He didn't slow until he reached the door farthest from his and on the right. He gestured for her to enter the room ahead of him.

Kate stepped inside. The dark floor was polished to a shine and showed no sign of wear. A small settee and overstuffed chair—also appearing unused—sat on a large round rug beside a warming stove.

The bed was a big four-poster with a high headboard and a flower-sprigged coverlet that matched the curtains. A tall bureau sat against one wall, a wardrobe on another.

Noah glanced around and set down her bag. "Marjorie keeps it clean."

"It's the nicest place I've ever stayed," she said with all sincerity and a touch of awe. "I've been in houses this nice when I delivered laundry, but I only dreamed of living in one."

Noah Cutter was obviously a very rich man. Land and cattle and a home like this. And Levi had been his only family.

"Rest," he said. "I'll bring water."

And with that he was gone.

Kate looked around the room, strolling over to peer at her windblown reflection in the mirror above the washstand. She removed her bonnet and absently tucked in stray hair.

A few minutes later he entered with a bucket and poured water into a pitcher on the washstand. Without another word, he turned and left, closing the door behind him.

After setting her bonnet down, Kate removed her coat and wandered to the window. In the yard below, she saw Noah stride toward the barn.

What a strange man.

What a strange predicament.

Removing the clothing she'd slept in, she used the water and a bar of lovely smelling soap she found on the stand. The ceramic bowl was so large, she stood in it and used the pitcher to rinse. The process wasn't as good as a bath, but getting clean felt heavenly.

From the stand, she gathered toweling that smelled of the sun and dried herself, then rummaged in her bag and donned clean underclothes.

After hanging the towels to dry, she tested the mattress, found it soft and comfortable and stretched out to rest her weary body.

Noah grabbed two full plates from the warming oven in the meal house and carried them to his kitchen. It was his habit to take his meal home and eat alone, and no one questioned the act now.

He didn't know what to do about Katherine, though. The house was dim and quiet, so he set their meals on the table and climbed the stairs.

At the end of the hall, he tapped.

Tapped again.

"Yes?"

"Supper."

"Oh, all right. I'll be down in a moment."

He struck a match and lit an oil lamp on the wall so she could find her way on the stairs.

True to her word, she showed up in the kitchen almost immediately. The wrinkled dress she wore had two rows of frills at the hem and another around the bodice, like something he imagined a young woman would wear to a summer picnic.

The only light came through the isinglass window on the stove. He pointed to a chair, and she sat.

Noah pushed a plate in front of her.

Katherine picked up her fork. "Thank you."

He sat at the opposite end of the table.

"Shall I light the lamp?" she asked.

"No."

"All right." She took a bite of the stew. "I guess I slept longer than I expected to."

"You were tired."

She nodded. "Perhaps tomorrow I'll have a chance to look around and meet some of the hands."

"Most'll be bringing cows down out of the hills."

"What for?"

"Branding."

"I see. I can do laundry, you know. It's what I do well—best actually. I won't mind taking over that chore."

"Marjorie earns extra doin' laundry. Wouldn't take her job away."

"Oh. Of course not. Well, I could make our meals. I'm not a very good cook, truly, but I can learn."

"That's Fergie's job."

"Oh." She glanced around the room, perhaps hoping to see something interesting in the shadowy corners.

"Coffee?" he offered.

"Yes. Thank you."

He got up, poured two tin mugs from the pot on the stove and sat one in front of her.

"I should be doing this for you." She smiled hesitantly and glanced up, but he turned away and strode to the far side of the table.

"Room all right?" he asked.

"The room is lovely, thank you. I guess it wasn't Levi's—I mean, since it'd decorated with flowers."

"No."

"Well, it's very nice. Thank you for the warm water, too."

He should have thought she'd want a bath and offered to fill the steel tub. "You want a bath, just ask. I'll fill the tub for you."

"Perhaps tomorrow morning. I would like to wash my hair."

He nodded.

"Anything you need. Clothing." He gestured helplessly, having no idea what women needed. "You can shop in Cedar Creek."

"I have two nice dresses." She flattened the ruffles at her bodice with a hand. "I was the smallest at the laundry when the owner didn't claim them. I suspect they belonged to a much younger girl, because of the ruffles, but nonetheless I was fortunate to receive such fine quality clothing."

"Uh-huh."

"What do you do here of an evening?"

"Work the stock. Tally the calves and accounts. Go to bed."

"I see."

"Books in the parlor. Help yourself."

She inclined her head in acceptance. Her thoughts traveled to Levi's body, which she'd overheard Noah telling the hands to carry to the dining room. "Will there be a funeral?"

"Visitation tomorrow. Levi's mother, Estelle, will be here. We'll bury him early Thursday."

"Oughtn't someone be sitting with the body?"

"Go ahead."

"I suppose you think it's odd that I haven't cried."

"No."

"I cried so much when Levi left that I guess I'm all cried out. That was five months ago. Maybe it just hasn't hit me yet that he's dead."

Or that he was with another man's wife, Noah thought. She'd barely fluttered an eyelash at that news. Maybe she was just a lot stronger than she looked.

Katherine stood. "I'll wash these plates."

"Set 'em outside the back door. Fergie'll get 'em."

She did as instructed.

Noah stood. "I have work to do. Good night."

"Good night."

He turned and entered the small room where he kept a desk and his ledgers and closed the door behind him.

Kate lit an oil lamp and carried it to the dining room, where she sat it on a long table that had been pushed to the side to make room for the coffin and an array of chairs.

She seated herself in the chair nearest the closed casket.

The baby chose that moment to give her a healthy jab and she covered the spot with her palm.

"I'm here, Levi," she said softly into the still room. "Your baby and I are here. At your home. Noah came to fetch me. He's a strange fellow, your brother. I still haven't had a good look at him. But he's very nice. And he's making a home for us. Like you were going to do."

She blinked and let her gaze travel the pine box. "Why didn't you come back? I thought you loved me." Her voice broke and her throat grew thick with tears. "I thought we were going to be a family. You said you'd find a job and come back for us. We'd have a fine house, you said."

She recalled what Noah had told her about a man named Robinson catching Levi with his wife. The pain of that betrayal had begun to sink in.

"What you did was wrong," she whispered into the still room. "You left me waiting. Were you ever going to come back? Were all those promises you made just lies?"

He hadn't even been where he'd told her he was going. He'd lied. And he'd left her. Played her for a fool. He'd been attentive and hadn't given her time to breathe when he'd been eager to kiss her and make love to her. She'd held out, sure that she wanted to be a virgin when she married.

And he'd asked her to marry him. Swept her off to a preacher and spoken the vows all pretty and nice. They'd spent two weeks together in his room at the boarding house, eating in the restaurant, making love each night. And then he'd started slipping away to play poker, staying out late and coming in drunk.

She hadn't been happy about that and they'd fought. For another week he'd stayed close, but then he told her he was going to look for a job. He needed to get away from the city, and there was nothing she wanted more, so she'd encouraged the plan. She'd cheerfully waved him off and watched for his return. He hadn't thought it would take more than a week or two.

Three weeks turned into four and she couldn't afford the room at the boarding house on her own. Kate got sick every morning, bleak evidence that Levi had left a babe in her belly. She'd set aside her pride then and asked her mother to let her stay with her until Levi came back.

Her mother had harped from day one that Levi was out for one thing and once he had it he'd be gone, and Levi's disappearance had been her opportunity to rub Kate's nose in callous I-told-you-sos.

Kate had swallowed embarrassment and clung to her hope that Levi would be back. Her time at the laundry and at her mother's was marked. She'd be leaving any day.

Each day her hope slipped a notch.

Each week her anger and shame increased.

Each month her desperation had grown until she didn't know whether it or the baby was feeding off her soul.

"You lied," she accused, her voice no longer wavering. "You used me and you lied. I want to forgive you. I should. I know I should sit here and pray for your soul and forgive you. But you know what, Levi? I don't forgive you."

She stood and turned her back on the coffin holding her husband's body. "I just might never forgive you."

And with that, she picked up the lamp and swept from the room.

Chapter Three

As he'd promised, Noah filled a tub of hot water for her the following morning. The shades were already pulled—she'd noticed he preferred them that way, and as he left the kitchen, he told her to lock the door behind him.

"Won't be back till evenin'," he said. "But Estelle will be here before long."

"I'll be ready," she promised. She locked the door, removed her clothing, then soaked in the deliciously hot water before washing her hair. Finished, she stoked the stove, combed out her hair and heated a flatiron to press the wrinkles from her dress.

She had donned it and was pinning up her hair when there was a knock at the door.

Kate unlocked and opened it.

A handsome woman wearing a black dress and matching hat held a vase of flowers while she looked Kate over from head to toe. She had graying brown hair and aristocratic high cheekbones. Her blue eyes widened when she noted the girth of Kate's belly. "Oh my!" She stepped into the room. "You're Katherine?"

"Yes, ma'am. And you're Levi's mother?"

Tears welled in the woman's eyes. She turned away, set down the vase and tugged off her black gloves. "I can't believe he's gone. He was my only child."

The complete lack of regard for her stepson struck Kate as insensitive, but she replied, "I'm so sorry for your loss."

She faced Kate once again. "You're with child?"

Kate unconsciously touched her stomach. "Yes."

"Noah didn't bother to tell me."

"He didn't know until two days ago. I don't think he knew about me until then. I'm not quite sure how he did know to find me."

"He said the men who…associated with Levi in Masonville told him where he'd find you."

"Oh. I see."

Estelle moved to the nearest window and opened the shade with a cluck of disapproval. "Can't have you sitting in the dark now, can we?"

"I just finished bathing and ironing my dress."

Estelle glanced from the tub of water to Kate's dress. Her mouth seemed pinched when she said, "Don't you have something black? You're in mourning, after all."

"This is my nicest dress. I know it barely fits now, but it's quite pretty."

"As my son's wife, you'll need appropriate clothing."

Kate looked down at her ruffled bodice and some of her optimism faded. Perhaps the dress was inappropriate for a widow.

The woman opened the door and hurried onto the back stoop where she rang the dinner bell.

Two hands came running as though there was an emergency. "Somethin' wrong, Mizz Cutter?"

"Come empty the tub before company arrives," she instructed.

They glanced at one another and lumbered forward.

"Harper Kimble," the man with a mustache

said to Kate as he passed. He wore fringed trousers and a red shirt with flowing sleeves.

"Kate Cutter," she replied. "Pleased to meet you."

"Newt Warren, ma'am," the other man said as he picked up a bucket. The two of them bailed bathwater and Estelle picked up the flowers and led Kate into the dining room.

After placing the vase on the table, the woman left the shades down on the other windows and lit candles, then moved to stand beside the coffin. "Why is it closed?"

Kate shook her head. "I don't know."

"Have you not looked upon your husband?"

She hadn't thought of it. Hadn't wanted to really. Noah told her he was in there and that was good enough for her. "No."

"Mr. Kimble! Mr. Warren!" Estelle called.

The two men appeared in the doorway.

"One more thing. Please remove the lid from my son's casket."

They moved into the room and Kate took a step back.

One man stood on each end and they lifted off the wood and set it against the wall behind

the sawhorses. With heads lowered respectfully, the men gazed upon the body.

"That will be all." Estelle waited until they'd
left the room before she moved to stand beside
the coffin. She trembled and raised a handkerchief to her eyes, sobbing out loud.

Kate's breath caught in her throat. She didn't
want to look at Levi, but couldn't help herself.
She gazed upon his handsome profile, noticed
the way his hair was combed uncharacteristi-
cally away from his forehead.

"He was a beautiful baby," Estelle cried. "A
beautiful golden-haired child and the most
handsome man. Isn't he handsome?"

Kate nodded. Levi had been handsome, no
question about it. Even his smile stole a woman's breath.

Estelle blotted her eyes and asked, "Who
dressed him?"

Kate peered at the dark suit Levi wore. She'd
never seen it before.

"I did." Noah spoke from behind them.

Startled, Kate turned. For the first time she
saw him without a hat. His chin-length hair
hung over the side of his face and combined
with his beard to hide his features.

The older woman turned and glared at her stepson. "You might have covered the sawhorses and brought in flowers. Is this the best you could do for a coffin for your only brother?"

Noah stared back at her. "Pretty 'im up, huh? Wouldn't change anything, would it?"

Despite the beard, Kate noted that his mouth turned up with an odd sort of grimace at the corner and that that side didn't move when he spoke. Perhaps that was the reason his speech sounded unusual.

"I might have known you wouldn't show him any respect."

"I loved him—I don't respect what he did."

Estelle cast him a censoring frown. "Are you going to speak of it in front of her?"

"She knows. Asked what happened and I told her."

"You might have spared her."

"Spared *you,* you mean."

"You're a dreadful man."

Shocked, Kate spoke up. "I made Noah tell me. I wanted the truth. He's been nothing but kind and considerate of my feelings and my well-being. You have no call to be angry with him, I assure you."

"You poor girl," Estelle said, moving to drape her arm around Kate's shoulders. "What a burden you've been given. First Levi's untimely death and then exposure to this heathen. You'll come home with me after the funeral tomorrow. I have room for you, and you won't have to stay here another minute longer than necessary."

"That's very kind of you. But I think this arrangement is going to work out just fine. I'd rather not live in town. Noah has my best interests at heart, I'm convinced."

"Don't be foolish, dear. You're understandably upset and you're not thinking clearly. You'll be better off with me—another woman. You'll be closer to the doctor and the stores and there are many social activities to help pass your days. I know firsthand what a dreadful bore it is being out here on this godforsaken ranch day after day."

Kate experienced a twinge of anger at the woman for supposing to know what she wanted and deciding what was best for her without bothering to ask. She didn't want to offend

Levi's mother, but neither did she want to have her choices made for her.

Her resistance seemed laughable, really, if she thought about it, because Noah had insisted she come with him, as well. But she'd *wanted* to accompany him. She did not want to leave with Estelle. "I'll remember your kind invitation if I should ever change my mind."

Estelle turned to glare at Noah. "That's my son's baby. You won't keep him from me."

Noah had turned to leave, but paused in the doorway. "No, that's Katherine's baby. The choices are hers."

He left and the two women exchanged a glance. Kate felt a surge of satisfaction because Noah had stood up to the woman on her account.

The sound of a horse and buggy prevented any further discussion as the first guests of the day arrived to pay their respects. Levi had been the son of a town founder, part owner of the Rockin' C, and townsfolk and neighboring ranchers trailed through for hours. As dusk settled, the string of visitors finally ended.

"Wasn't it odd that Noah didn't attend all day?" Kate asked Estelle. She had met dozens of curious strangers, some she sensed were only there to look around, but Noah had kept his distance.

"The man's not fit for society and he knows his place," she replied.

"What do you mean?"

"Even his own father couldn't bear the sight of him."

"You make it sound as though Noah is some kind of monster."

"Indeed."

"I've noticed his speech is odd. What I can see of his mouth looks somewhat…different."

"Hideous, you mean. As is his entire face."

"What's wrong with it?"

"An accident scarred him. Don't make me talk about him—it's too unpleasant. We've plenty of dishes to choose from for our supper. It's so kind of the ladies to bring gifts of sympathy. Let's set the kitchen table and dine now, shall we?" She opened a cupboard. "Not a decent piece of china in the entire house." After looking over the items to choose from, Estelle selected two chipped plates and arranged place settings.

"What about Noah? You've only set places for two."

"He won't join us. He eats alone."

"He ate with me last night."

Estelle gave her a surprised glance.

Noah entered the house at that moment, his hat low over his forehead.

"Will you be sharing our meal?" Kate asked hopefully.

He glanced at Estelle, then at the two plates on the table. "No."

"Please?"

Kate's soft plea stopped him in his tracks. He turned to eye her.

"Please join us," she said again.

Ignoring Estelle's scowl, he took off the hat and hung it beside the door, then turned back and seated himself at the far end of the table.

Quickly, Kate got another plate and more silverware and set it in front of him. Moving close to do so, she noted the back of his right hand, dark from the sun, but ridged with a jagged pale scar. What kind of accident had scarred his hands and his face? A fall from a horse? They weren't burns.

"Mrs. Krenshaw brought buttermilk," she said cheerfully. "Do you like buttermilk?"

He nodded without looking at her, and she poured a Mason jar full to set in front of him.

After taking the warmed casseroles and dishes from the oven, she served Noah and then she and Estelle seated themselves.

"Katherine will need appropriate clothing," Estelle said brusquely. "Black for mourning and material adequate for the coming months. I will take her to Annie Carpenter's place. Annie still sews for a select few women, and she's the best seamstress in a hundred miles." To Kate, she added, "Comes from a fine family, Annie does. The Sweetwaters have a lovely home. Annie married the blacksmith. Her parents weren't too happy about that at first, but he provides well for her."

"I don't want to be a burden. I can work to pay for my own clothing." Kate looked to Noah. "I can take in laundry if you don't mind me using your tubs. I see there's a fine room in which to do the chore. I could have more clothesline strung."

"Certainly not," Estelle answered immediately. "Cutter women do not take in laundry.

You're Levi's wife and as the mother of his child, you're entitled to privileges. This ranch provides more than enough to meet your needs."

"I wouldn't mind, really." Estelle made it sound as though there was shame in the task.

Noah finished a bite. "Don't recall ever agreein' before, but Estelle's right. You don't need to take in laundry."

Estelle bobbed her head as though punctuating his speech. "You see? I'm right."

Kate stared at her plate, wishing she knew a way to earn her keep that would be acceptable to these two. As much as they seemed to detest each other, they both wanted her with them and wanted her taken care of. "I'm fortunate that you both care so much about my well-being and that of my child. Thank you."

"You're welcome, dear," Estelle replied.

Noah finished his meal without another word. When he was done, he rose and shut himself in his little room.

"Boorish man," Estelle said, picking up plates.

"I'll get these," Kate told her. She had already seen Tipper carry a valise up the stairs and had surmised that Estelle was staying the night.

"You go up and rest. Tomorrow is another full day, and you want to be fresh."

"Yes, thank you. You're very thoughtful. Good night, dear."

"Good night."

Since Noah wasn't there to insist she set the plates out of doors for someone else to wash, Kate took care of them.

Afterward, she took her coat from beside the door and escaped out into the cool night air. The darkness and quiet were complete and all-encompassing out here in the foothills. Kate walked away from the house and stood beneath the night sky where she took a deep, cleansing breath. Everything was clean here. New. She had a fresh start.

She sensed more than heard someone approach and turned to discover Noah's broad form in the moonlight.

"You all right?"

"Yes, I'm fine. I just came out to enjoy the sky and the air. It's so fresh, don't you think? Better than perfume. Better than clean laundry. I can smell blossoms. I wonder what they are. Have you ever smelled anything equal to this? Just look at the sky. It goes on forever, doesn't it? I feel like a little speck way down here on the ground."

"She upset you?"

She glanced at him. "Estelle? No, she's been very kind to me. She's anguished over losing her son and that's understandable. I feel bad for her."

He grunted.

"You two are not close."

He looked across the dark pasture. "My father married her when I was eight. Had her own child soon and never had much use for me. She didn't like this place, wanted a house in town."

"But this is such beautiful country and the house is perfect. I can't imagine anyone not loving it here."

"Estelle hated that my father built the house for my mother."

"Oh, I see. That's a shame."

Amazingly, Noah offered more information. "She stayed awhile after Levi was born. But as he got older, he wanted to work the horses with us. She moved to town."

What kind of mother left two children behind

so that she could live in a nicer house? "When did your father die?"

"Several years later."

"I never knew my father. After Mama married him, he got gold fever. He lit out for the gold fields when I was little. Mama never had much use for men after that. Justified, she was, because of having to raise me all by herself and all. I always hoped for something better. A whole family."

She didn't mention Levi's name, but the hurt of his betrayal was there in the things left unspoken.

"You're thinking I didn't do too well choosing a husband and a father for my baby," she said softly. "And I expect you're right. Taking a husband is kind of like finding an egg in a nest."

He cocked his head and looked at her.

"You know it's a bird in there, you just don't know what kind it'll turn out to be."

"Can usually tell by the shell what kind of bird it is."

A breeze blew a strand of hair across her face and flattened her skirts to her legs.

"I like April," she said, undaunted by his

pragmatic contradiction. "It's full of promises. The snow's nearly all melted and flowers are just beginning to bloom. You know summer's coming and soon there will be plenty of sunshine. Summer's not pretty in the city. There's lots of smoke and dust and it's mostly hot. I'll bet it's nicer here. I read a book once where the boys went fishing in a pond and caught their own fish for supper. Do you catch fish?"

"Sometimes."

"Where at?"

He pointed. "Lake yonder. Or the river."

"Would you show me sometime?"

He nodded.

She wrapped her arms around herself. "It's going to be a good spring and an even better summer."

"When's the baby comin'?"

"August I expect. I think that will be a good time. Better than winter. Won't have to bundle him up or keep him out of drafts and such." She turned and looked up at his shadowed features. "Noah?"

He jerked at her address. "Yeah."

"I was wondering…that is, were you hoping I'd say yes and go with Estelle? I mean, it's a bother having me here, and you don't even know me. I wouldn't think poorly of you if you'd just as soon I not be here."

"You'n the baby are better off here."

He hadn't said he wanted her here, however. He felt a responsibility, though, and for now his sense of duty was her salvation. "I'm grateful," she said softly.

"Go to bed now."

"All right." She headed for the house, sensing him behind her. He remained on the back stoop while she entered the kitchen and hung her coat. She dipped a pail of water, gave him a little wave through the screen door and headed up the stairs.

Kate slept amazingly well under Noah's roof. Though it was a strange place and a completely new environment, she felt safe and comfortable. She woke rested and felt somewhat guilty over the fact when she saw Levi's mother.

Estelle had dark rings under her eyes and her face seemed puffy. After breakfast, she donned a hat with a black veil that shaded her eyes and gave her a dramatic sorrowful air, which Kate suspected had been her intention.

Kate wore her other good dress. It looked

similar to the last, except that it had an inch of lace that showed at the hem and at each sleeve. Estelle had shaken her head upon seeing it, but commented that there was nothing to be done about her costume that day.

Noah wore dark trousers, a jacket with the collar turned up and a shirt and string tie. A black felt hat shaded his eyes.

Newt and a fellow they called Jump came to nail the lid on the coffin, carry out it out and place it on the back of a wagon.

Within the hour, townspeople arrived, along with the preacher. Kate met Marjorie Benson, a tall woman with friendly brown eyes and a big smile. The crowd walked behind the wagon, which Noah guided to a grassy area. Piles of rocks indicated other graves.

"Who else is buried here?" Kate asked Marjorie.

"The senior Mr. Cutter and an old drover that I know of."

A hole had already been prepared for the casket. The people gathered and four men lowered it into the grave. Kate got a sinking feeling at the permanence of the act. Levi had been her husband for such a brief time. All these folks had known him longer than she. But she carried a part of him inside her. A baby he'd left her before he'd run off and taken up with another man's wife. How many of these people knew that part? she wondered. Thinking of it, Kate felt used and of little value.

Reverend Davidson read from the Book of Psalms and said a prayer. Estelle sobbed woefully and dabbed her nose with a delicate lace-edged hankie. Two sympathetic women friends braced her on either side.

From under the brim of her bonnet, Kate studied faces. Some were curious, others were filled with empathy. Noah's was shaded as always. He stood apart, his chin down and his right hand in his pocket as it had been during the entire service.

When the praying came to an end, Noah, having pulled on a pair of gloves, stepped forward, took up a shovel and began to move earth from the mound beside the grave into the hole.

Kate's eyes filled with smarting tears. She wasn't sure if she was crying for Levi, for herself or for Noah who determinedly covered the wooden coffin with dirt.

Marjorie gave her a sympathetic hug. "You

poor dear, so young—much too young to be a widow. Noah is gruff and seems unreachable, but he'll do right by you. I trust he will."

Kate nodded. She believed that, too, or she wouldn't have been here.

Kate didn't know how she endured the day. It lasted forever and the house and yard were continually filled with strangers. She was introduced to Eldon and Mildred Sweetwater and learned that Eldon and his son Burdell were the town bankers. Burdell's wife, Diana, was a lovely woman with two children.

Annie Carpenter was the seamstress Estelle had told Kate about, and she was married to a blue-eyed man named Luke. Estelle made a point of telling Annie that they would be visiting her for a wardrobe soon.

"I have two ladies working for me now," Annie told them. "So we should be able to handle your clothing needs quickly."

Kate met the Renlow family, nearby ranchers who were also related to the Sweetwaters. So many curious and assessing gazes were cast her way, she felt like a two-headed calf in a carnival.

At one point Kate looked out over the array

of buggies and wagons, the smatterings of folks engaged in conversation beside makeshift tables of food, and imagined herself instead at the lake Noah had told her of. She pictured a smooth, placid body of water, turquoise like the river that flowed down from Indian Peaks, with soft grass along the banks and mounds of clover in which to lie back and gaze at the clouds.

Noah had disappeared once people arrived and swarmed over the Rockin' C like ants on a cake crumb, and she couldn't blame him. Wherever he was, she'd bet it was a far cry better than being here.

Kate ventured around the side of the house to escape the press of neighbors. Along the entire north side lay a garden in early spring garb. Rocks had been used as curving borders along the beds. The ground appeared freshly turned around the plants. Kate couldn't name most of the greenery, but she recognized the rosebushes planted in abundance.

What a lovely sight this must be when the buds came into bloom! The garden lay just below the triple floor-length dining room windows and would be beautiful even from inside.

She planned to throw open the windows and smell the roses once they bloomed.

Noah, a gardener. It was difficult to imagine.

At last gathering her resolve, she returned. Eventually the ranchers and townspeople expressed their sympathy for the thousandth time and bid their goodbyes. Estelle accepted a ride from Dr. Martin, wedged her valise in the back of his buggy and rode off with a wave and promises to return and assist her newly found daughter-in-law.

Kate entered the kitchen, where dishes had been washed and stacked and the table was laden with food in various containers and wraps.

She hadn't been able to eat more than a few bites all day, but she still wasn't hungry. She was exhausted to the very marrow of her bones, however, so she climbed the stairs, removed her shoes and dress and fell onto the bed in a heap.

It was dusk when a rap at the door woke her.

Kate sat up, disoriented for a moment, and then the room and the day rushed back into her mind. She gathered a folded quilt from the foot of the bed around her and padded to open the door.

Noah stood holding a plate of food and a mason jar filled with milk. "You should eat."

She stepped back. "I suppose I should. I do feel a little hungry now, thank you."

He didn't enter.

"Have you eaten?" she asked.

"Doin' that now."

"If you don't mind, I'll dress and come down to join you."

He nodded and turned away. His boots sounded down the hall and then on the stairs.

Kate donned her dress, then took a few minutes to brush out her wildly mussed hair and braid it. She left the braid hanging loose and found him in the dimly lit kitchen.

"There were certainly a lot of folks here today," she said, taking a seat and picking up the fork he'd placed beside her plate. "That says a lot about the respect for your family."

"I run a big spread. Spend a lot of money in town."

She eyed him. "None of them are your friends?"

He shook his head.

"Why not?"

He shrugged and ate.

Kate sampled one of the casseroles on her plate. "Do folks know? I mean, about how exactly that Levi was killed?"

"I didn't tell 'em. Estelle sure won't."

"But gossip will travel, don't you think?"

"Can't say."

She picked at her food again. "Who planted the rosebushes on the side of the house?"

The fork paused on its way to his mouth. He lowered the bite to his plate. "My mother had a rose garden. It was overgrown and full of weeds when I thought to save it a few years back. I sent for more bushes."

"The garden must be lovely when it's in bloom. I can't wait to see it. And the smell— why, it must come right into the house and fill every room."

"Uh-huh."

"Too bad they aren't blooming yet. We could have placed some on the grave today. The preacher did a good job, don't you think? The prayer was especially touching."

"Not much for prayin' and the like."

"You go to church on Sundays, don't you?"

"No."

His reply caught her by surprise. Her mother

had always taken her to church and nearly everyone they knew attended. "Are you a heathen, then? You don't believe in God?"

"I believe in God. He's not the problem."

"What is the problem?"

"People."

"Oh." She'd heard how Estelle spoke of and to Noah, but surely not everyone shared her low opinion.

"You go," he said. "Ride with Marjorie and Tipper."

"Sunday's still three days away," she replied. "I have time to think about it. Everyone stares at me…." She shook her head to dismiss the thought.

Noah laid down his fork. "You have nothing to be ashamed of."

Tears smarted behind her eyes. She blinked to keep them from falling, but the attempt was useless. She'd been foolish to fall for Levi and everyone would know it soon enough if they didn't already.

Noah felt more awkward than ever at Katherine's distress. She had loved his brother. He understood because he had loved him, too, but Levi's callous behavior stuck in his craw. It took only the smallest thing to please Katherine. She was delighted with flowers and stars. Sunsets and good weather fairly made her delirious. So far he hadn't heard her speak of anything that she couldn't paint in cheerful colors.

It would have been so easy for Levi to make this woman happy. Why the thought angered him more than any other, he didn't know. Maybe because without the least effort Levi could have had everything Noah could never hope for. And he'd thrown it all away. Got himself killed and left a wife and babe behind.

Katherine's silent tears were far more eloquent than Estelle's histrionics. Noah was completely at a loss as to how to react to a crying woman. Though they shared the loss, they were strangers. He could think of nothing to say that would change anything or bring her comfort.

So, as usual, he said nothing.

Chapter Four

Kate was grateful that Estelle didn't come to the Rockin' C on Friday. She used the reprieve to rest and to learn the layout of the house and outbuildings.

At noon Fergie brought her a bowl of stew and a chunk of bread.

"What is everyone doing?" she asked.

"Roundin' up cows and branding," he replied. "Takes weeks in the spring."

She saw Noah only at supper when he brought two plates of food from the meal kitchen.

"I could cook you supper whenever you like," she told him.

"No need to double the effort. Fergie cooks every night."

The beans were tasty and the golden-baked corn bread was perfection. She couldn't have done half as well. Noah couldn't realize the wise choice he'd made in declining her offer.

But she felt the need to contribute.

Noah had placed a crock of butter and a jar of jelly on the table near her, then dipped portions onto his plate before seating himself at the far end. Kate thought eating together would be nicer and simpler if they sat closer. She moved the crock and jar nearer him, moved her plate, then took the chair to his right.

"I was surprised the first time I saw that whole crock of butter on the table. Estelle had to tell me to help myself."

He stopped eating.

She glanced at him.

He lowered his hands to his lap without looking at her.

Kate reached for the butter and spread some on her warm corn bread.

"This is a treat," she told him. "At home we rarely had butter. It was too expensive to buy from the general store. Estelle said someone on the ranch probably makes this."

"Fergie."

"I would enjoy seeing how he does it." She noticed that he hadn't picked up his fork and resumed eating. Setting down her slice of corn bread, she dropped her hands to her lap. "Have I done something wrong? You didn't want me to sit here, did you?"

Quickly she got up and took her plate back to the opposite side of the table. "I just thought it would be easier to talk. I'm sorry."

She'd lost some of her appetite and her cheerful mood faded. The fact that he didn't want her near made her feel as though she wasn't good enough. Surely he hadn't intended to make her feel that way, but it was her impression all the same. "You've been very generous," she told him softly. "I'm grateful to be here and I'll try not to step over the boundaries."

He picked up his fork and held it suspended a moment before finishing his meal. It was difficult to be in his company when she couldn't see his expression or read his eyes. He shut himself completely away from her and obviously preferred it that way, so she'd just as soon get used to it.

When he was done eating, he got up and went back outside.

Kate washed and dried the dishes, then wandered the house. She found the books he'd told her of and selected one. She'd been reading in the parlor for an hour or so when the back door opened and closed and the sound of another door indicated he'd shut himself in the back room. She shouldn't feel slighted. The man hadn't asked for her company and was generously sharing his home. He didn't have to like her or to spend time with her. Kate took the book upstairs and read until she fell asleep.

Saturday was no different from any other day of the week. The men did the same chores at the same times. But that night after Fergie prepared supper in the meal house, Kate learned that most of the hands left the ranch for the evening.

Marjorie sent a message with Tipper that Kate was welcome to ride to church with them the following morning. Kate decided she would enjoy the outing and the company, so she accepted.

She had washed and dried her good dresses, and now she heated the flatiron and pressed the rows of ruffles until they stood out like new. She hummed as she worked, and the words to the song came to her unconsciously.

Noah stood on the porch listening to Katherine sing. Her voice was as pure and sweet as the woman herself. After having her in his home all week, he was still astounded at her dauntless cheer and optimism. Being in her company, he felt like an ugly wormhole on a rosy apple.

Standing in the darkness, he didn't have to see her to picture her hair in the glow of the lanterns, tresses as rich and thick as honey. In the sunlight it shone with a life of its own. Her eyes were dark with emotion and sparkling with life. She had skin as smooth and pure as fresh cream. Looking at her was like squinting at the sun on a bright day. Her prettiness was so good and so warm that it hurt.

Sometimes he wondered how Levi had met her. At the laundry, he supposed. He'd probably invited her to dinner or for a carriage ride and had easily won her heart. The marrying part confused him still. Levi hadn't been one to stay in one place or to commit for longer than a few weeks at a time. Noah had raised countless puppies and even a raccoon that Levi had brought home and quickly lost interest in. The hound that followed him around the ranch now was the whelp of one of Levi's strays.

This was different. This wasn't a pet he'd tired of feeding and cleaning up after. This was a woman who needed provision and protection. A woman *and* a child. When Noah thought about the baby, he couldn't help wondering if a baby would find his appearance frightening. Or since the child would be exposed to him from an early age, would he simply accept Noah's appearance? It seemed logical that a baby would be more tolerant than adults.

The child would eat at Noah's table and learn to ride his horses and grow to manhood on the Rockin' C.

A corrective wave of caution followed that thought. Or womanhood. The baby could be born a female. If so, Katherine would do all the raisin'. He didn't know the first thing about females.

Secretly he hoped Katherine's baby was a boy.

"Have you ever known Noah to attend church?" Kate asked Marjorie the following morning as they sat together on the wagon seat.

"Never," she replied. "He doesn't attend anything where folks are gathered. Doesn't even come to town if it's something the hands can take care of."

"Can't be healthy, staying to himself like that for his whole life. Folks need friends."

"Been that way as long as I've known him."

They arrived at the little white church and Marjorie introduced Kate to a few parishioners she hadn't met at the funeral.

As soon as Estelle saw Kate, she bustled over. She was dressed in black from head to toe, and her expression did not convey pleasure at seeing Kate. "You'll sit with me, dear."

Marjorie gave Kate an encouraging smile and took a seat with her husband.

Estelle led Kate up the aisle to one of the first wooden pews. "I'll speak with the Bensons after church and see to it that one of them brings you to town tomorrow. We can't have you dressed like that—you're a Cutter now. We have an early appointment with Annie for measuring. She'll have fabrics and patterns for us to go over."

Kate smoothed the dress Estelle so obviously disdained over her lap and folded her hands.

"You need gloves, too. A lady always wears gloves in public. I've invited the Huttons to have dinner with us after church. Walter is Copper Creek's schoolteacher and his wife, Rose, helps with Sunday school. They are a lovely couple."

Preacher Davidson greeted them on his way to the pulpit and within minutes the service was under way. It was much the same as the church Kate had always attended with her mother, except that they had always sat in the rear with the laborers. It seemed the folks were divided in this congregation, as well. The Sweetwaters, who Kate knew were bankers, sat in the front and the hands from the Rockin' C were in the back of the room.

She had the feeling that she should be sitting back there with them, but Estelle had practically nailed her to this pew.

After the service, Estelle was greeted by neighbors, and she made a point of pushing Kate toward them as though insisting they accept her. Kate recognized more than a few odd glances and took note of whispers behind gloved hands.

Annie Carpenter made a point of drawing her away and saying hello. She held a bright-eyed toddler she introduced as her daughter, Rebecca.

"I didn't know you had a child." Kate smiled at the chubby little girl. "She's beautiful."

"We'll have another one in the fall," Annie told her.

Her smile told Kate that learning a baby was on the way hadn't struck terror into her heart as it had hers.

"And you have time to sew, as well," Kate said with admiration.

"That's why I need help now," Annie said. A pretty dimpled young woman joined them. "This is my cousin, Charmaine Renlow."

Charmaine's eyes widened when she met Kate. "Oh my! You're living out on the ranch with Noah Cutter? Aren't you frightened?"

"Why, no."

"I've heard frightful things about the man. Some of the stories say he hunts with his bare hands and eats raw meat."

"That's ridiculous," Kate replied, offended for the man who'd been so kind to her. "He eats the same as everyone else. And it's all cooked by Fergie."

"I've never seen him up close," Charmaine added with a conspiratorial whisper, "but they say he's hideous to look upon."

Her words confirmed what Estelle had told Kate, though she hadn't had a straight-on good look at him herself. She couldn't really deny what she wasn't sure of. But she could certainly attest to his character. "He's one of the kindest men I ever met. I suspect much of the talk has been aggravated above the truth."

"For your sake, I hope that's so," Charmaine said sweetly. A young man approached then and she blushed at his arrival. "Katherine, this is Wayne." An unexpected Southern drawl laced Charmaine's tone as soon as he joined them.

Wayne nodded at Kate politely. "How do, Mrs. Cutter."

No one had ever called her Mrs. Cutter before and she glanced aside for Estelle before she realized he had referred to her.

"We're having dinner with my parents this afternoon," Charmaine told her, and slipped her arm into the crook of Wayne's. "And a croquet match. I'm going to let him win this time."

Estelle found Kate and took her arm then, and Kate wished the young people a goodbye. Their way of life was as far away from hers as the sky was from the ground where she walked.

She'd spent her growing-up years laboring to make money for food and a place to live, and she'd earned her way by washing clothes for people just like these. She'd be willing to bet these young women had never had to want for anything. They went directly from comfortable homes with their parents to good marriages.

Kate didn't begrudge them a thing. She simply had nothing in common with them.

Or with Estelle and the Huttons as it turned out. Estelle's cook had prepared rack of lamb, string beans and something called a Caruso salad with lettuce, tomatoes and a tangy sweet fruit topped with paprika and oil dressing. Kate speared a piece of the fruit. "What is this?"

"Why, it's pineapple, dear," Estelle replied.

Kate closed her eyes. "It's incredible."

"You've never tasted pineapple before?" Rose Hutton asked.

"No, ma'am. I expect there's a lot I've missed. But I'm enjoying learning now."

"I'm trying to convince Katherine to live here with me," Estelle told the Huttons. "She seems to feel an unfounded obligation to Levi's step-brother."

Estelle's home was elegant, no doubt about

it. Kate had never seen furnishings so plush or rooms so ornate. Everywhere she looked there was another painting or vase or Oriental rug or brocade settee. But none of the rooms seemed as comfortable or as welcoming as the room Noah had given her. The opulence here didn't appeal to her as much as the serenity of the ranch house she wanted to think of as her home. She didn't want to have to explain her reasons to Estelle again. She'd already told her she didn't want to live in the city.

She couldn't think of much else to say that afternoon. The time seemed to drag. Once the Huttons had gone, Estelle sat her down in the parlor. "There is talk," she said.

"What kind of talk?"

"About you being on the ranch alone with that man."

"We're not alone. There are hands."

"Not living in the house, there aren't. It simply isn't proper. You shouldn't be living alone with him."

"I guess I don't know much about proper. All I know is he's kind and I like living there."

Estelle clearly didn't approve of her reply. When she had her groomsman take Kate home,

Kate was grateful for the escape. If that's what Sundays would be like, maybe she didn't want to go to town in the future.

She changed into a day dress and read in her room for an hour or so before she went downstairs and found a tin of tea. She had just brewed a pot when Noah entered the kitchen.

"Good evening. Would you like to join me for a cup of tea?"

He glanced at the pot on the table. "All right."

She took out two cups and poured the tea, setting one at the spot he preferred.

He took a seat.

She studied his carefully averted face, wishing she could see him better. "Sugar?"

"Yes."

She watched him dip a spoonful and stir. Picking up the cup, he took a sip. Raw meat indeed.

"I saw many of the folks who were here for Levi's funeral today. Most were friendly. Some stared and whispered though. I met Annie's cousin and a fellow named Wayne. Appears they're sweet on each other."

He acknowledged her chatter with a nod.

"Estelle's home is lovely. Her cook made us

an elegant dinner. Lamb, can you fancy that? And I tasted pineapple for the first time. It's the sweetest fruit I've ever had.

"The hillsides between here and town are bright blankets of purple aster. It's early for those, don't you think?"

As though he thought he should reply, he said, "Might be early."

"Estelle made us an appointment tomorrow with Annie Carpenter." She set down the cup she'd been holding. "I have to confess that I'm not entirely comfortable about having a lot of new clothing made for me."

"You need clothing."

True, she didn't have dresses to fit her growing figure, but the garments certainly didn't need to be expensive. She wouldn't be wearing them but for a few more months. "I was thinking I could ask Annie to show me how to help her and I could do some of the sewing myself."

"Estelle sets store by Annie's work."

"And I'm sure it's worthy of the praise, but I could make up for some of the cost by helping."

"Don't bother yourself over the cost of a few

dresses. If Estelle didn't say it plain enough, I will. You're a Cutter. We will take care of you."

Kate rested her hands in her lap. "It's just not what I'm used to. I'm sure you can understand."

"Your life has changed."

She tipped her head in reluctant acquiescence. "Yes."

He stood. "Thanks for the tea."

"I found it in the cupboard."

He dipped a pail of water and left the room. Minutes later, she heard his boots on the stairs.

Kate cleaned up the few dishes and extinguished the wall lantern before dipping her own water and climbing the stairs.

She studied the crack of light under Noah's bedroom door as she passed, hurrying on to her room.

She closed herself inside. She hadn't been uncomfortable staying here this past week. She hadn't felt unsafe—quite the opposite, in fact. An enormous portion of her burdensome worries had been lifted and even breathing seemed easier now. She could actually see past the pressing momentary need of each day and look to the future.

She didn't need people putting thoughts in

her head, making her question, making her wonder even more about Noah. Most of the local gossip was hogwash, she'd already discovered.

But she wasn't so sure about propriety. About their living arrangement being fodder for more talk. She knew her staying here was fine and innocent, and she couldn't help what others thought or said. Even Estelle, and Estelle knew better.

That night when Kate climbed into bed it was with a dent in her formerly oblivious pleasure at having a home.

She had trusted Levi, too.

It had only been a week since she'd learned of Levi's death, Kate thought. One week and now here she was standing on a stool in Annie's dress shop, listening to talk of silks and taffetas and comparing hues of green and violet. Annie had taken her behind a screen where she now stood perched in her chemise and drawers. A lot of good the screen had done, because Estelle popped her head around and gasped. "Good Lord, what on earth are those?"

Kate looked down at her underclothing. "My unmentionables, of course."

"How can you even sit still with that dreadful jersey next to your skin? Annie, she will need underclothing, as well. I knew it, of course, but this—well, *this* is an emergency."

"Actually, I have some lovely pieces made up and for sale in the bureau out front. Why don't you look through and see what will fit?"

Annie met Kate's eyes with an expression of sympathy. "She means well," she said softly.

Kate nodded. "Oh, yes. I'm not offended. I didn't have much to pack when Noah came to get me, and I'm seeing now that it was no way to live. I knew, of course, but having never seen the other side of things, it wasn't quite so plain as it is now. Every day I'm overwhelmed by the abundance I see and by other's generosity. Sometimes I think I should pinch myself to make sure I'm awake, but if I'm not, I don't want the dream to end. Have you ever felt anything equal?"

"I have. It's the way my Luke makes me feel."

Annie's comment about her husband touched Kate immeasurably. She wondered how it would feel to be confident in a husband's love. "Where's Rebecca?"

"My mother adores staying with her for a few hours while I come to the shop. They're probably having a tea party on the lawn. When's your baby due?"

"August, I think."

"I don't envy either of us the summer days in the heat," Annie said in a sympathetic tone. "But you'll have your baby months ahead of me." She held a silky wrapper out to Kate and Kate slipped it on. "Let's go look at fabrics. You'll want more than black."

For the first time Kate noticed an awkward gait when Annie walked. Whatever caused it didn't seem to hamper her abilities.

Estelle was piling chemises and drawers and petticoats on the counter in a frenzy. "All of these. And will you make a few in light blue?"

The pile was bigger than all the clothing Kate had ever outgrown in her lifetime. "Whatever will I do with all those?"

"You need several changes and enough so that you can pick and choose when some are in the laundry," her mother-in-law replied.

"Do *you* have this many underthings?" Kate asked Annie in an aside.

"I'm sure I do. And Charmaine has even more. Why, the girl has so many clothes, she can't wear them all." She smiled. "We females are entitled to our little pleasures."

A loud clap of thunder startled all of them.

Estelle scurried to the front window. "Goodness, it's turning dark."

An immediate sense of alarm washed over Kate. All thoughts of pretty-ribboned chemises flew from her head. "I'd better get back to the ranch before the storm hits."

"Maybe you should stay with me," Estelle suggested.

"No, Tipper and Marjorie will be waiting. They went for supplies and said they'd be back for me." She found her dress and Annie helped her into it. The fact that Kate was more willing to face a storm than stay with Estelle said more than the woman would ever know.

"I think I'll close the shop and go get Rebecca and take her home," Annie said.

They said their goodbyes and Kate found Tipper and Marjorie waiting outside, the bed of the wagon covered with a tarp. "I have an extra tarp in case we get caught in the down-pour," Marjorie called.

Tipper helped Kate to the seat and they headed out of town.

Angry black clouds moved across the sky and shadowed the landscape. Before long it looked like twilight rather than midday. Jagged streaks of lightning periodically pierced the ominous sky and lit the mountains in a brief eerie glow. Perhaps it was the elevation or the open land-scape, but everything about this storm seemed louder and more intense than bad weather ever had in Boulder.

Anxiety tensed in Kate's body. She didn't like storms. Never had. Everything about the darkness and the power of the wind and lash-ing rains sent shivers of terror along her spine. She told herself it was foolish, that storms came and spent themselves and moved on, but that didn't seem to help at the moment.

She put on a brave face, held tight to the wagon seat and prayed they'd arrive at the ranch soon.

Rain pelted them before they got close. Marjorie opened the tarp and the three of them huddled beneath it. The women's skirts were drenched by the time they reached the Rockin' C.

Noah, with rain drizzling from the brim of his hat, met them in the dooryard. The barn doors were swung open wide and Tipper drove the team right inside.

Kate smelled the animals and hay and felt the warmth of the building. A small measure of comfort replaced some of her anxiety. Newt and Jump unharnessed the team as Noah reached up for her.

His bare hand was warm and strong, with calluses against her palm. She felt safe with her hand in his. He let go, however, and reached to grasp her around the waist and lift her down as though she weighed no more than a child.

Thunder shook the rafters at that moment. She jumped, her heart hammering wildly, and tucked herself against his side.

It happened so quickly, neither of them was prepared. She looked up. He looked down, and their eyes met. Lightning flashed through the open doorway, illuminating them where they stood. His eyes were brown, like polished mahogany, and fringed with black lashes.

Thunder followed and her body tensed involuntarily.

He steadied her with a hand at her waist and another on her shoulder. With fascination, she watched his mustache move as he said, "It's okay."

She became aware of the others—Marjorie climbing down behind her, Tipper moving to peel back the tarp from the wagon bed, Newt and Jump talking to the horses and each other. Cold rain dripped from Noah's hat brim to her shoulder.

Embarrassed at her childish fear, her face grew warm and she backed away from his tentative hold. "I—I'm sorry."

"You're cold," he said. "Go change." He plucked a slicker from a nearby post and handed it to her.

She draped the oilskin over herself and hurried out. Thunder cracked while she was midyard and just that quickly the rain turned to hail. With a shriek, she ran to the house, balls of ice hitting the ground and bouncing, pelting the oilskin over her head.

From the relative safety the kitchen, she stood, slicker dripping on the floor, heart pounding, and stared at the scene outside. The sky was a deep green-gray, a color she identified with terror. Wind blew wet leaves and howled through the branches of the nearby trees. Pellets of ice covered the dooryard in a white blanket

Shaking with cold, she forced herself to remove the slicker, hang it on the back porch and close herself inside. She fed kindling and wood to the stove, then ran up and changed into dry clothing.

Noah, too, would be soaked when he came in, she thought on her way back along the hall. His door stood open, so she entered. The room she'd never seen before was furnished with a bed, a bureau, an armoire, a washstand and an overstuffed chair that looked to have held Noah's form many nights. In the bureau drawers she found clothing, and hurried down to hang her wet dress and stockings on a line behind the stove. Hail hit the metal stovepipe in a deafening torrent.

With trembling hands, she made a pot of tea and sipped a hot cup. The warmth helped soothe the shakes that racked her body, but the hail and wind kept her stomach in a knot. Noah would want coffee when he came in, so she measured grounds and boiled water.

Eventually there was a thump on the back porch and the door burst open. Noah struggled out of a pair of wet boots. He hung his hat and rubbed his hands together. "No more work today. I need to get into dry clothes."

"I fetched clothing down for you. It's in your room—back there."

He looked surprised, but nodded his thanks and went to change. After hanging his own clothing beside hers on the line, he glanced toward the stove.

He poured a cup of coffee, added sugar and sipped it standing up. "Heck of a storm brewin' out there."

"Did Marjorie go home?"

He shook his head. "Stayed to help Fergie with supper."

"What do you do when it storms like this?"

"Anything. Nothing. Stock still needs fed." He unbuckled his holster and laid the .45 on the table, then brought a rifle, rags and oil from the back room. He sat at the table and methodically took the guns apart and cleaned them.

The hail stopped and the sky lightened to gray while he worked. The steady drip of rain was less frightening than the wind and hail.

Kate had finished the first book, so she found another and sat at the table in the glow of an oil lamp to read.

Eventually, Marjorie brought a kettle of roast, potatoes and carrots, enough for several people. "Will you and Tipper eat with us?" Kate asked hopefully.

Marjorie glanced at Noah.

He nodded. "Stay."

She and Kate set the table and Marjorie went to find Tipper. They took seats, Noah deliberately isolated at his end and the others on the opposite.

It was obvious that Noah wasn't comfortable with the Bensons there, but he wasn't comfortable with her, either, so she enjoyed their company.

"I think we should make the ride home while there's a break in the clouds," Tipper said once he'd finished eating and gone to look out the door.

"Go," Kate assured Marjorie at her look of uncertainty. "I can do these few dishes by myself."

Marjorie glanced at Noah, who waved her on, so she wished them a good night and left with her husband.

"I have to check the barns." Noah walked out behind them.

He didn't return until long after she'd finished the dishes and taken her book upstairs. She read until her eyes grew weary, then turned down the wick in her lamp and snuggled into the covers.

The wind came up again, buffeting the house and rattling the windowpanes. Kate told herself there was nothing to fear. Wind and rain made a lot of harmless noise. But talk to herself all she would, nothing calmed her nerves or her shaking limbs. She'd been this way since she was a girl and a storm had whirled into Boulder with a vengeance.

That particular day Kate's mother had left her home alone while she'd worked at the laundry. Frightened at the lightning and thunder, Kate had run all the way to the laundry house only to find that the workers had taken shelter in a storm cellar and that no one occupied the wash rooms.

In the yard, shirts and trousers whipped in the wind until the lines snapped and clothing spiraled in a frenzy. Terrified, Kate had clung to a clothes pole. A wet sheet tore loose from its mooring and caught on her, wrapping her head to toe. Thunder crashed through the heavens. No one heard her screams or came to comfort her. When the storm had finally passed, workers discovered her, and her mother had punished her for not staying home.

It had happened years ago, but the day was as clear in her memory as if it had been yesterday. Kate could still see the ominous green-gray sky, hear the howling wind and feel the claustrophobic press of the cold wet linen that wrapped her head and body. All it took was rain and thunder and she was shaking like a baby again.

She couldn't bury her head, that was even more frightening, so she buried herself to her chin and curled in a ball in the center of the bed. That had been a long time ago. Children grew up and overcame their fears.

Bright white illuminated the room in a jagged

flash. Kate braced herself for the rumble of thunder that followed, and when it came, it shook the house.

Another flash, this one accompanied by a loud cracking sound, made her sit bolt upright in bed. This time when the thunder rolled, it came with the sound of breaking glass. Kate watched in horror as the entire window beside her bed crashed inward and a huge branching shape invaded the room with a swishing noise and a spray of rain water.

Kate shrieked. Thunder rattled again and this time the sound was on top of her because the window was gone and part of a tree lay across her bed.

Through the dark, wet branches, she could see the flicker of flames dancing outside. She thought her heart would burst from her chest.

Chapter Five

"Katherine!" Her door burst open. Noah took one startled look at the scene and shot to her side. "Are you all right? Are you hurt?"

All she could do was cry.

He peeled the covers back from her as far as the branches would allow and glass fell away. Gingerly, he lifted her in his arms and carried her down the hall.

In his room, he placed her on the bed, lit two lamps and carried one to the night table. With infinite concern, he took each arm and inspected it through her cotton gown, then looked at her feet and ankles, studied her face and checked her hair and scalp. "Do you hurt anywhere?"

Kate had calmed minimally. His anxiety over her welfare touched her heart. The shock had begun to wear off as soon as she noticed he wasn't wearing a shirt and that the hair that usually hung over his eye was tucked behind one ear.

Noah's chest was a mass of V-shaped and ragged scars. The sight and the thought of the pain he must have suffered gave her a physical ache. In her shock, she placed a hand to her own breast and her gaze traveled upward. The skin beside his eye was puckered and pulled the lid downward slightly.

But his eyes. His eyes were kind and full of concern.

She wanted to cry for him. Tears smarted behind her eyelids.

"Katherine, are you hurt?" he said more forcefully.

She shook her head and whispered, "No."

He realized then. She knew the moment the awareness flooded over him. His posture stiffened and he took a step backward, holding up a palm. "Stay right here."

Without turning his back on her, he moved away and yanked a shirt from a hook by the door and donned it, missing buttons in his haste. Hobbling into a pair of boots, he ran out and down the stairs. The commotion outside and orders being shouted registered dimly.

An accident, Estelle had said. What kind of accident scarred a body so severely? Numb now, she glanced around his room, got up and fed wood to the warming stove and climbed back on the bed.

After several minutes he returned, his hair and shirt damp, the muscular contours of his upper body illuminated by the lantern. "Lightning struck that big old tree. Rain put out the fire. Men are covering the hole best they can till morning."

He took the towel from the nightstand, dried his hair and face, then returned to study her where she sat in the middle of his bed. "You're shaking."

"I'm afraid of storms."

He pulled up the covers, urging her to lie back, and added another blanket from a chest at the foot of the bed. "You can sleep here if you feel safer."

"What about you?"

"I'll take the chair," he answered.

"That won't be comfortable."

"Want me to leave? I can put you in another room."

She sat up quickly, ashamed of her childishness, but unwilling to stay alone. "No. No, don't leave. Please."

"I'll change into dry clothes, then."

She turned away and listened to his clothing rustle. A moment later, he settled into the chair.

He meant to stay. She lay back down and pulled up the covers. The sheets smelled like cedar.

"I've been afraid since I was just a girl." She told him the story of being caught in the storm and wrapped inside the sheet for the duration. "Ever since then I try to tell myself rain is just rain, but I can't help what happens to me."

"A tree coming in the window didn't help," he said.

"Thanks for letting me stay with you. It's a comfort to have you here. Comforting to be here, too."

A few minutes passed and the only sounds were his pocket watch on the bureau and the now distant rumble of thunder. In the lamplight, Noah studied the curve of her cheek and the shadow of her lashes. He imagined what her cheek would feel like if he stroked his finger across it.

The image of his scarred hand near her perfect face was too ugly to entertain, so he dismissed the fantasy and looked at her small form lying in his bed. A tremor of sexual awareness ran through his body, shaming him for its crudeness. She was as trusting and pure as anyone he'd ever known, and thinking of her presence in a lustful manner was wrong.

He'd never had a woman in his bed before.

He'd never had a woman.

Noah didn't want to think of Levi touching her, kissing her, making love to her. The image disturbed him, and he couldn't get past the conclusion that Levi had taken advantage of her.

She was sweet and wholesome and undoubtedly ignorant of men like his brother. Of men like himself, for that matter. If she thought he even *imagined* anything sexual about her being here, she would be out that door and down the road, storm or no storm.

He extinguished the nearest lamp and left the one on the bureau burning. Katherine's braid trailed across his sheets like a thick rope of honey-colored silk. Her creamy-white cheek lay upon his pillow. He imagined the rest of her tucked so cozily in his bed—slender limbs, curving hips, soft breasts and the swell of her belly.

It had all happened so fast, but he'd carried her against his bare skin from her room to his. He'd felt her delicate frame and soft form in his arms and against his chest.

His chest. He'd been in such a panic to reach her that he hadn't grabbed his shirt. If she'd been halfway coherent at all, she had seen him. He'd seen her shocked expression. The thought made him feel sick.

Perhaps the shock had been from the storm and the breaking window, he tried to convince himself. After all, she hadn't mentioned it—and she talked about everything.

"Noah?" she said softly, breaking the silence.

"What."

"What happened to you?"

She had seen. His world curled protectively inward. He'd never let anyone see. He'd never been careless. Hiding was as natural as breathing. He glanced at her, but she wasn't looking at him. Her eyes were closed as though life and its meaning didn't hinge on his reply.

And at that moment he realized that, for her, it didn't. She hadn't lived her whole life in this body, cringing from prying eyes and curious stares. She had told him everything about her, frank as you please. She'd shared her childhood, her misery at being left in Boulder and the dread she felt when she thought she might have to raise her child there. She'd told him about her love of the stars, her fear of storms.

He could tell her something, too. "I was thirteen," he began. He'd never told anyone before. Never said the words. His throat felt tight. "My father and I were stringing barbed wire. A wire snapped and it wrapped around me."

Just words. Just words, but so much more. So much pain and shame behind them.

"Cut me all over. Cut a nerve in my face. My father had to snip and pull the wire away to get me free. That hell took forever. I was covered with blood. So was he."

"You must have been so afraid," she said softly. "And hurting so much."

He didn't remember the pain much. He remembered the horror on his father's face. And the guilt. And the way the man never looked at him again after that. For all the rest of his father's years, he had been so repulsed by Noah's appearance that he'd never looked straight at him again.

Estelle had always talked about Noah and how repulsive his appearance was as though he wasn't there. As though he'd died. In some warped way her treatment had been easier to bear than his father's.

Katherine sat up. "I'm so sorry."

At the sound of her voice, he realized how much he'd revealed and looked at her.

There were tears in her eyes and on her cheeks.

Something in his chest ached when she'd spoken those words. Some indefinable thing that made his heart beat faster and his stomach feel as though he'd been kicked by a horse. He was wearing a shirt and he'd let his hair fall back over his face, but he'd never felt more exposed. "It was a long time ago."

"But it seems like yesterday. I know."

"Tonight," he said. "I thought the window glass had cut you." The worst thing he could imagine.

"I'm fine."

"I must have scared you, yankin' you out of bed and touchin' you all over like that." Touching her—talking of touching her gave his heart a jolt.

She shook her head. "Quite the opposite. I was never so glad to see someone."

He let that statement settle in his mind. He didn't think anyone had ever been glad to see him before. But she hadn't meant it literally. She'd meant she'd been glad to have someone come to her rescue. No one could be glad to see him.

Katherine lay back down and pulled the covers to her chin, nestling into his bed. "Thank you for telling me."

Sometime later, she slept. Noah got up quietly to check the room at the far end of the hall. Harper and Lucky had covered the exterior with tarps to prevent rain from pouring in, but the bed was already wet and leaves and glass covered the floor and mattress. It would take extensive work to fix this mess.

But Katherine was safe, and that was all that mattered.

Kate woke to the sounds of breaking glass and hammering. She discovered herself in Noah's bed and sat up in the rays of sunlight that streamed through his window.

A pail of water had been set at the foot of the washstand, and her wrapper along with her clothing was strewn across the foot of the bed. Noah had gathered all her things and brought them in here, and she had slept right through it.

She washed and dressed and pinned up her hair before realizing he'd forgotten her shoes.

She made her way down the hall toward the noise that emanated from her room. The tree was gone from the opening, but the gash in the wall where the window had been broken and the frame torn loose let in sun and a bee or two.

Wearing a pair of gloves, Tipper had all the glass swept into a pile and was using a flat tin dustpan to scoop it into a bucket.

The bed frame sat empty, the mattress and bedding gone.

"Marjorie's been waiting for you to wake up," Tipper said. "Noah wants you to go to town with her today."

Kate soon learned that Noah wanted her to finish her fittings and clothing selections, as well as go to the mercantile and search the catalogs for new wallpaper and furnishings for her room.

"Noah, I don't need new furniture," she argued as they stood in the shade beside the porch.

"Baby needs a crib. A bureau for his things. Might as well do a room for him and fix up your own, as well." His eyes were shaded from her by the brim of his hat as usual, and she wished she could see them. It was frustrating to not be able to see his expressions.

"If you won't pick 'em, I'll have to let Estelle. You may as well have what *you* like, rather than what she thinks you should have."

She absorbed his words. "When you say it like that, I guess I don't have any choice. I don't think I'd want anything Estelle chose.

But it's not necessary. My room is fine just the way it is."

"No. Wallpaper got wet last night and needs replaced. I'm done arguing. Get what you want."

She glanced up to where one of the hands stood on a ladder hammering the window frame into place. "I didn't come here to change things."

He followed her gaze. "Some things need changin'."

She looked at him, at the puckered skin near his eye. He ducked his head. Impulsively, Kate stood on tiptoe and reached up for his hat. She pulled it to the side and away, baring his head.

He was so surprised, he only stared at her, but by then the corner of his eye was covered by his dark hair.

"It's purely irritating not to see your eyes when we're speaking. Half of what a body's saying is in his expression and his eyes."

Beneath his sun-darkened skin, she thought she detected reddening. She hadn't meant to embarrass him.

Before she could say more, he grabbed his hat from her grasp and jammed it back on his head. "Buy the paper. Buy the furniture and order whatever you need for the baby that the mercantile doesn't have in stock. Buy fabric for baby things. You said you could learn to sew, so have Annie show you how to do that."

Taken aback by his gruffness, Kate merely shrugged.

He turned and stalked away.

"I didn't mean to make you mad," she called after him.

He kept going.

She spent the day in Copper Creek as he'd ordered. Estelle showed up at Annie's and added to the orders for clothing. Using the excuse of needing to give Rebecca a nap, Annie invited Kate home, and it gave the two young women time alone.

While the little girl slept, Annie showed Kate how to make gowns and nappies and blankets. Besides her services and her knowledge, Annie offered friendship, and Kate gladly accepted it. She'd never known this privileged life and all that it offered, but she was quick to embrace it.

She was making a new life for herself and making sure her child had all he'd need. It wasn't the life she'd imagined with Levi, but it was better than she'd known until now.

Her temporary room was across from Noah's and was the bedroom that had been Levi's. She lay in bed that night and tried to capture something of her husband. But it was just a room, and one he hadn't spent much time in for years. Sometimes it was hard to believe she'd been married to him. Sometimes it was hard to remember him.

The next day Annie and her mother, Mildred, met Kate at the mercantile and helped her choose wallpaper and pieces for the two rooms. As she told Noah about her selections that evening, she noted that he listened to her without lowering his head or looking away. One hard-won day at a time, he was letting go of years of inhibition. He seemed to sense that his hands and face made no difference to her. She liked him for his kindness and quiet strength, and if they were to be a family, she wanted him to be comfortable with her.

By the end of the week, Kate's window had been repaired and the floor refinished, though Kate hadn't seen much wrong with it to start with. She chose not to attend church that Sunday, because she didn't want to spend another afternoon with Estelle.

Obviously offended, Estelle drove out to the ranch that afternoon.

Kate made tea and served it in the parlor.

The woman sipped primly from the cup. "I was quite disappointed not to see you in church this morning."

"I made the ride to town several times over the past week and wasn't up to another one." It wasn't a lie really. She hated to lie and wasn't very good at it.

"Citizens of our standing need to keep up appearances."

Appearances. Apparently, Estelle set store by what people saw and thought of her and her family. The fact that she was ashamed of Noah didn't set right in Kate's yaw.

Kate endured her company until finally the woman must have felt she'd accomplished what she'd come to do by plying guilt tactics and said, "I'm going to speak with Noah before I leave."

Kate watched Estelle march across the dooryard without finding her stepson. She came back and rang the dinner bell. Several hands ran to answer the emergency call, and she sent Jump to fetch Noah.

Noah strode from the barn to stand beside her buggy. The driver was sitting on a tree stump petting Noah's hound dog.

"I understand you're furnishing a room to her taste," Estelle said.

"Yup."

"That's probably a wise idea. You should have her do the entire house."

"Can if she wants."

"Do you think that's enough to keep her here?"

He cocked his head at the question.

"What *is* going to keep her here? She loved Levi. Levi's gone. What if she meets a man? Someone in town."

Noah had been staring across the pasture, but he turned to glare at her.

Estelle's cold blue gaze bore into his. "She could remarry and take Levi's child away."

He hadn't thought that far ahead, hadn't wanted to. Hadn't had the courage to. Noah would never have children of his own. Levi's child would be the one to inherit all of Rock

Ridge and the ranch. It made him sick to think of Katherine finding a new husband.

She was young and beautiful and any man would want her.

"It's too soon for her to think like that."

"For now. But what about next year? Or two years from now? She'll grow to hate this place."

"She won't," he denied.

"You don't know that. You don't know what will happen or how she'll change or who she'll meet."

"What do you want me to do?"

"Think about marrying her yourself."

"What?"

"Don't look so surprised. She needs you right now. She needs what you have to offer her and the baby. You won't get anyone else to marry you. I'm not saying she'll jump at the chance to marry a crude man, but she is unrefined herself. The security you can provide should be enough."

Noah's ears rang as he tried to absorb Estelle's notion.

"She's not worthy of the Cutter name," she said with a disdainful sniff, "But she is having

Levi's baby. Make her see that keeping Levi's child here is important."

Estelle hadn't spoken this many words to his face in twenty years. Yet the words she chose still had the ability to inflict wounds. Her speech and the fact that she wanted to manipulate him and Katherine to suit her own selfish desires angered him. "What do you care?"

"That is Levi's child she's carrying. I will not lose the last of my family."

"I can't work up any pity for you," he said. "You left two boys out here to be raised by our father while you went to live in town."

"I had only one son." Her cruelty never wavered.

"And look how he turned out."

"Don't you dare speak ill of Levi."

"Oh hell, no. The man was a saint."

In a huff, she gathered her skirts and called to her driver. "You're obstinate and ugly as always, but you know I'm right. Changing the subject to make it look as though I'm in the wrong doesn't change the situation or what needs to be done. You know what you need to do."

"I need to wash my ears out with lye after listening to you."

The driver helped her into the buggy where she adjusted her skirts. The horse pulled the rig away.

Noah watched the plume of dust in its wake and tamped down the anger and resentment she always dredged up. The woman reminded him of the serpent in the Bible stories where personified evil spoke to man and put doubt in his head. She had always made him feel ashamed and unlovable, and though he was a grown man, her disdain still wounded.

He went about his chores thinking of Katherine. Was he providing enough reason for her to stay? What if she did meet someone?

Fergie had taken the afternoon and evening off, so Kate sliced ham and made sandwiches for their supper. They drank milk and ate canned peaches. Noah glanced at her from time to time. He didn't have to see her through another man's eyes, because his own told him well and good what an appealing sight she made.

That night as he lay in bed with her across the hall, his mind conjured up dozens of scenarios. He saw himself teaching Levi's young son to ride and rope. The boy would be accepting of Noah's looks, as Levi had been. Noah still hoped that by exposure from infancy, the child wouldn't fear him. He pictured them eating meals together as a family and the child learning to read and write of an evening.

Then, thanks to Estelle's vile suggestions, Noah saw a man entering the picture. He cataloged the young men he barely knew, the widowers, imagining one or more of them seeking out Katherine. Who would it be? Someone handsome and charming. Someone who could win her heart and who would ask her to marry him.

She would be a beautiful bride.

And then—he would take her away. Noah would be alone again. No young voice. No slates on the table. No marbles or toy horses scattered around.

It was a dramatic scenario and he was only torturing himself with the sensational images. But he knew he didn't want her to take away his nephew. And he didn't know what would make her stay.

The more he thought about Estelle's suggestion, the less wild it seemed. It was a plus that Katherine didn't cringe at his appearance, didn't show her revulsion. But marrying him? It was one thing to sit across the table from him or to look at his eyes when they spoke. It was an entirely different thing to expect her to share a room. A bed. And he wouldn't expect her to do either.

Tomorrow was a new week. He had much to do finishing both rooms, and here he was lying awake conjuring up impossible dreams. Noah scoffed at himself and diverted his thoughts to cows. Nice, safe cows.

Two rugs were delivered early in the week. The following week wallpaper arrived. That Thursday the furniture came and by Friday the rooms were finished.

Noah stayed away from the house while workers from town were there, but came to help Kate arrange the pieces to her liking and hang new curtains.

With a tiny floral-striped print on the walls, lace curtains and a solid mahogany headboard and chest of drawers, her new room suited her. It was cheerful and pretty, yet not frilly or overdone. She'd also selected a chest that stood at the foot of her bed. Annie had given her drawings of flowers and she'd framed and hung them. A cradle padded with white blankets stood nearby.

The baby's room was a pale yellow, with an iron crib, a chest of drawers and a rocking chair. Noah had taken it upon himself to order a rocking horse and to build shelves for toys along the wall under the window. The shelves also served as a bench.

As they studied the layout together, Kate was overwhelmed by the enormity of the changes in her life and by Noah's generosity.

"I feel I should be doing more." She blinked back tears. "You've done all this." She gestured with an inadequate sweep of her arm. "And I've given so little."

He raised his chin to look at her. He'd left his hat downstairs, something he did more and more often around her, and she could plainly see his eyes and the scar that puckered the outside corner of the left one. "There's something more you can do."

Kate's spirits soared. Noah was finally going to let her contribute something. She smiled with pleasure and faced him, her hands clasped together in expectation. "What? Say it. Anything you'd like. I do so want to be more important, to feel as though I belong."

"You belong," he assured her. "Don't doubt it."

She took a seat on the bench by the window and smoothed the fabric of the black dress she wore over her knees. "Don't keep me waiting. What is it you'd ask of me?"

Noah averted his face. Dimly she recognized the instinctive action resulted because she sat in front of the window, and the light would surely strike his face if he looked directly at her.

He raised his chin and stood with both feet solidly planted on the new rug. "Marry me."

Chapter Six

Kate blinked a few times, mentally adjusting her hearing and her comprehension. She must have heard wrong. She flattened a palm to her chest. "Noah?"

He backed up a step but looked directly at her. "You're my brother's wife. We can make a new family. Raise his child together. I don't expect love. This isn't about that. This is about the baby. About family."

"Well. Let me catch my breath and think." Absently she fingered a tendril of hair that lay against her neck. "The idea's not outlandish. Fairly common probably, and people do marry for worse reasons."

She stood and moved to stand at the other side of the room, so the light would be behind him and he'd feel comfortable looking at her.

"This is what you want?"

He seemed to consider his reply for a moment. "According to the Bible it's a man's duty to take his brother's widow."

She would just as soon have heard him say it was what he wanted, rather than his duty, but she couldn't afford girlish fantasies or fanciful expectations. Her life was about survival, not dreams.

He had told her she was welcome here forever, but if they became man and wife, her place would be wholly secure. Her baby would be provided for and have a stable home to grow and learn. Rock Ridge would truly be their home. Should she trust that he meant what he said?

"The ranch will be your son's," he told her, as though interpreting her silence, "whether we marry or not."

"What about you?" Another thought had occurred to her. "Was there anyone before I came? I wouldn't want you to be sorry you married me because you felt it was your duty to your brother. All this time I've just assumed you had no plans and no special woman in your life, but I haven't asked."

"There's no one," he assured her.

"Perhaps in the future? You could meet a woman more suitable. It's plain I don't have many skills for living on a ranch."

"No one," he said again. "I don't want to hire you as a hand, I want to take you as a wife."

Take you as a wife. Her heart fluttered at those words. She'd never felt like a man's wife before. Except for the intimate parts, she supposed. But Levi hadn't thought enough of her to provide for her. He hadn't even stayed on or been faithful. Noah would take the commitment seriously. He'd already seen to her welfare in dozens of ways. She wanted to truly be a man's wife. To truly belong and have a home.

"My answer is yes, then. It's what I want, too."

He looked surprised, as though he hadn't expected her to agree at all, especially not so quickly, and his expression worried her.

A sudden concern gave her pause and she took a step forward. "You did want me to say yes, didn't you? If you were just asking because you thought it was the right thing to do and you were hoping I'd say no, that wasn't how I took it. You were very convincing and—"

He held up a hand. "I wanted you to say yes. It's only one word."

"All right. Yes." But she couldn't stop at that. "This was unexpected, but I know it's the right thing. As long as we've made up our minds, we ought to just move right ahead, don't you agree? When shall we do it, then?"

"We only need the reverend and witnesses."

She nodded. Plenty of women married immediately after being widowed. Especially if they had children who needed provision. She wanted to tie up this agreement as soon as possible, but she didn't want to make more out of it than it was. "I'm in mourning, so it should be quiet and simple."

"I'll talk to Reverend Davidson right away."

"Estelle," she said, suddenly thinking of the woman. "She doesn't approve of me. Will she object?"

"No."

"How can you be certain? Well, I guess there's nothing she could do anyway. Is there?" Glancing down at the dress she'd worn because Estelle insisted it was proper, Kate had another question. "She won't expect me to wear black, will she? I have so many new dresses. Annie just finished an especially pretty one."

"Wear any color you like. It's your day."

A nervous flutter dipped in her chest and she smiled. Her day. Her wedding day. It wouldn't be that different from the day she'd married Levi in front of a justice of the peace, but at least this marriage would be spoken over by a preacher. She prayed what she'd seen of Noah's character was true and that her future would be more secure. How could she be certain? She'd learned the hard way that nothing was ever guaranteed. But this was her best opportunity and she would think positively.

"May I carry flowers?"

"If you wish, certainly."

"May I ask Annie to attend? She's the nearest thing I've ever had to a friend, and it would be such a delight to have someone there who wishes me well."

Noah didn't appear too pleased at that request. She remembered Marjorie's statement that he never went to town. Even at Levi's funeral he had stayed to the side and then disappeared for the duration of the day. Expecting him to appear in front of a gathering in church was out of the question.

"I have an idea," she said. "Why don't we have the service here? The parlor is large enough for a few guests. We could hold the ceremony of an evening, rather than during the day when folks need to work."

By planning the event indoors and in the evening, she could control the situation so that the room was lit by only one or two lanterns and not overly bright. Noah would be much more at ease.

"Would that be acceptable?" she asked eagerly.

He nodded. "Yes."

"Will we invite Estelle?"

"Not on my behalf. Do you want her here?"

She shook her head in relief.

The next few moments were awkward. Kate suspected a good many engagements and weddings were planned without romantic trappings or feelings of any kind, but she felt as though the two of them should seal this important agreement some way.

Impulsively she stepped forward. Raising one

arm to Noah's shoulder, she stretched up on tiptoe so she could kiss his cheek.

"Your beard tickles. I didn't know what it would feel like."

His body stiffened and he said nothing.

"I'm going to look through my new dresses and decide which one I'll wear." She turned and practically floated from the room.

Noah's face was warm and he could still feel the touch of her lips on his cheek. He raised his fingers to the place where she'd pressed a kiss. Katherine was unlike anyone he'd ever known. But then, he'd never known a woman before.

Sometimes he wondered if there was something wrong with her vision, but obviously there was not—she described everything she saw and did in vivid detail. And she *had* seen his hands and his chest and his eye. Only a small portion of his face was visible above his beard, but she had asked him about the scars.

So she could see well enough, but she had little reaction—something he wasn't used to.

He didn't need defending, but she took his side when speaking to Estelle, and that was amazing in itself.

She had accepted his proposal of marriage,

a marriage without love or physical attraction, and she hadn't had to think long about it. She needed the security, just as Estelle had predicted. Noah had planned to entice her, and it had worked.

And then she'd intuitively understood his reluctance to appear in public and had, without direct mention, asked to be married here. In the evening. Conditions arranged to his unspoken preference.

A feeling like a yawning hunger pulled in his chest. She had the ability to humble him. Not shame him. Never to shame him. This was a new feeling. And it would take some getting used to. He hoped the feeling—and Katherine—stayed and that he had a chance to get used to both of them.

Without wasting any time, Noah saddled a horse and rode to Copper Creek. It had been a while since he'd set foot in town, and he avoided the main street, riding out of his way to approach the preacher's from the opposite direction.

A plump woman in a flowered dress and starched white apron stepped out onto the porch at his arrival. He dismounted, tied the bay to a hitching post and stood at the fence. He never got close to people. From that distance, he appreciated the display of climbing pink roses that arched over the porch entrance.

"I don't believe I've had the pleasure," the woman called with a friendly dimpled smile.

"Noah Cutter, ma'am. I'm here to see the reverend."

"Come inside." She gestured to the brick path between them. "He's having his afternoon coffee."

Noah didn't want to get any closer and he definitely wouldn't enter the house. If he did, courtesy would dictate he remove his hat. He took a few steps, but his gait stalled. "Won't take but a minute, ma'am. If you'd ask him to step outside, I'd appreciate it."

"I make a good cup of coffee and there are fig cookies," she told him. "But I can serve them up out here equally as well. You wait just a minute, Mr. Cutter." Turning, she opened the screen door and entered the house.

He glanced up and down the street, relieved to find it empty of travelers or neighbors.

He pulled on his gloves and walked toward the house.

A few minutes later Preacher Davidson came out in his shirtsleeves. "How do, Noah?"

Noah climbed the stairs and shook his hand. "Well, sir."

The preacher had glanced at his gloved hand, but said, "Have a seat."

Noah wasn't good company, didn't have any practice at social activities, so he looked at the chairs before deciding he had no choice. He perched on one.

"You picked a beautiful spring day to come calling," the man said cordially.

"I want to get married."

The preacher's eyebrows rose. "You always were a man of few words. That's a sign of wisdom, according to the book of Proverbs. Well, well. Married. Now that's news. Can I assume you have a wife picked out?"

Noah nodded. "Katherine."

"Levi's widow. I see. You two have talked this over and decided it's for the best?"

"She's having a baby."

"Bless her heart. I didn't realize. You and I

spoke very little at Levi's funeral as I recall. Shame losing your brother so young like that." He shook his head sadly. "And she's lost her husband. But marrying you is a wise choice to be sure. You're a fine rancher and a good man, as was your father. Even if you don't attend services." He winked.

Noah wasn't sure what he could say to that. "A week from tonight would be good. I'd be obliged if you would come to the Rockin' C to marry us. And obliged if you don't mention the plans to anyone."

"Keeping it small," Preacher Davidson said with a nod. "It would be my pleasure."

The preacher's wife came out with a tray holding cookies and cups of coffee. She set the tray on the round wooden table and offered a cup to Noah.

He didn't reach for it. "Thank you, ma'am, but I can't stay. Reverend."

She exchanged a glance with her husband. Noah got up and touched his hat brim briefly, then hurried down the stairs and untied his horse. He swung up onto the saddle and urged the animal into motion.

* * *

That night as they ate supper, Noah, seated as usual on the far end of the table, told Kate what he'd arranged. "A week from tonight. The preacher will come."

Kate laid down her fork. "That's perfect, isn't it? I want you to be easy with the plans."

Noah had never been easy around anyone except Levi in his entire grown life, so he didn't hold out much hope for next week. But it was the best that could be arranged, so he nodded.

The following day Noah instructed Harper to drive Katherine into town so she could invite her friend Annie and make arrangements for anything she needed.

Charmaine was present in Annie's shop, sewing seed pearls on an ivory gauze veil. "I've been working on this veil for a month," she told Kate. "I was hoping it would bring me luck. Wayne has mentioned to friends that he is going to ask me to marry him." She released the veil and shrugged with both palms up. "So far, he hasn't."

"That's perfectly exciting," Kate told her. "You two make a charming couple."

Charmaine's cheeks blushed prettily. "Why, thank you!"

"Join us for tea." Annie gestured to a chair and brought out a china teapot and delicate cups. "I don't have any more of your dresses ready yet. Have you decided on some changes?"

"No, this isn't about clothing. I've come to share something." Kate's palms grew damp with nervous anticipation. And now that Charmaine was here, it would be rude not to include her in the invitation. "And to ask you to come out to the Rockin' C next Friday evening." She glanced at each woman. "Both of you."

"What's the occasion?" Annie asked, handing her a cup.

"Noah and I are going to be married."

The needle stilled in Charmaine's fingers. She glanced up at Kate with surprise. "Married? You're going to *marry* him?"

Kate nodded.

"Are you sure you want to do this?" Charmaine asked.

Kate raised her chin a notch, wishing now that Annie's cousin hadn't been present and that she hadn't felt impelled to include her.

"Luke and I will be honored to attend," Annie responded quickly. "Thank you for thinking of us."

Kate smiled with relief at her acceptance and sipped her tea.

"Thank you for the invitation, Kate," Charmaine said, touching Kate's hand. "I will be pleased to come."

Kate turned over her hand to grasp Charmaine's. They looked into each other's eyes a long moment. "There's obviously something the rest of us don't know about the man," Charmaine said finally. "Because I can tell you're satisfied with this decision."

Incredibly relived at her intuitive understanding, Kate told them, "He's the kindest person I've ever known. He grows roses, can you fancy that? He's been treated unkindly by his stepmother and stared at by strangers and neighbors his whole life. He considers his appearance intolerable to others and avoids people. It's sad, don't you think, to have spent so many years hiding?"

"Yes," Annie agreed. She took a seat beside Kate. "I know what it's like to have people looking at you and thinking you're different."

"Annie's parents kept her in a wheelchair for years," Charmaine told her. "She didn't get to go to school or attend gatherings. It wasn't until she met Luke that she realized she could do more than they had ever allowed her to do. She started walking and had to defy her parents to marry Luke."

After hearing her incredible story, Kate admired Annie all the more. "I feel bad now." Kate set down her cup. "I imagined you'd always had an easy life. But I guess none of us really knows what the other has gone through."

"Oh, I was spoiled and had an easy life," Annie said. "Too easy. I was so pampered and coddled that I felt like a china doll on a shelf. That's no way to live. I love having a full life. Being a wife and mother and running my shop."

"Her life makes the rest of us yearn for something equal," Charmaine said in her dramatic way. "Luke adores her. He's loved her since she was ten years old and he was fourteen." She proceeded to tell about the way Luke and Annie had met at Annie's tenth birthday party, how Luke had taken her for a ride on his horse, and how Annie's brother had beaten the tar out of him afterward. "Isn't that the most romantic thing you've ever heard?"

"It is indeed." Kate had never heard a story so touching. She couldn't help comparing Luke's devotion to his wife to Levi's abandonment. Annie was fortunate to have a husband who loved her.

"Charmaine, perhaps we shouldn't be reminding Kate of what she's lost," Annie said softly. "She's a widow, after all."

Kate sniffed and Annie found a handkerchief for her. "I'm not one to feel sorry for myself, really I'm not. I'm sorry."

"It's your delicate condition," Charmaine said. "Annie cried at the drop of a hat before Rebecca was born."

Kate couldn't resist a chuckle at their sympathetic words and expressions. She'd never had girlfriends, had never known the pleasure of feminine sympathy or understanding. "Now that I think back and think hard, I'm not so sure how I truly felt about Levi. He promised to take me away from Boulder and my work at the laundry. I think I was in love the idea of escape. I believed I loved him or I wouldn't have married him, would I?"

Kate gathered her courage and spoke the truth. "I hadn't seen him for nearly five months when he was killed."

"What do you mean?" Annie asked.

"He went to look for work and a place to live and didn't return."

"He owned half the Rockin' C—why would he need work and a place to live?" Charmaine asked.

With the truth spelled out so plainly, Kate knew with certainty that Levi's promises had been lies and his plan to find work merely an excuse to leave. If he'd loved her, had wanted her as his wife, he'd have brought her to Rock Ridge. "It was a lie," she replied.

He had wanted to make love with her and she had refused because they weren't married. So he'd married her. After a few weeks, his itch had been scratched and he'd moved on. Her humiliation was a burning ache in her stomach. And now she was entrusting her safety and that of her child's to another man. She tamped down her doubts. Noah was not Levi.

Annie scooted close and wrapped her arm around Kate's shoulders. "Everything's going to be fine now." She patted her back. "You have a home with Noah and he will take care of you and your baby."

"Yes," Kate replied. She returned the hug and they separated. Imagining Noah taking care of her was overwhelming. The whole idea of being married to him was overwhelming. She had so many questions in her head that she had to fix her mind on something else. "I have a newly papered and furnished bedroom and the baby's room is charming. I can't wait to show you."

"You'll show us Friday?" Charmaine asked. "What are you going to wear?"

"One of the dresses Annie made for me is a shimmery pale green. I was thinking I'd wear that one."

"I saw that—it's beautiful." Charmaine reached for the veil she'd set aside. "Kate, I'd like for you to have this."

Kate blinked in surprise. "But that's yours. You were making it for good luck and you've put so much work into it. I couldn't possibly accept something so…so special."

"You're the one with a wedding planned, so

perhaps it was good luck, after all." Charmaine grinned. "Maybe Wayne will get an idea when he hears of your wedding. I can always make another."

Kate knew the cost of the materials and seed pearls was more than she'd earned in a month working at the laundry. It was a more generous gift than she'd ever been offered. "It's so beautiful," she said, her throat thick with tears. "I've never had anything as pretty."

Charmaine placed the veil in her hands. "If we apply ourselves for the next hour, we can have the rest of the pearls sewn on."

Kate accepted the gift and the young women's friendship with a hopeful heart. These two accepted her as an equal and had taught her the joy of sharing and the blessing of genuine concern. Preparations for this wedding were as different from her first as night and day.

The day Noah had brought her to Copper Creek had been the most fortunate day of her life. She would remember who she had to thank for changing her existence. She would strive to make certain his life was better because she was here. She would show her appreciation in all the ways she possibly could.

While they worked, Annie helped her with a few ideas for the ceremony and offered to bring a cake. Kate rode back to the ranch feeling good about the plans.

She had no particular duties around the ranch or the house and was chastised at every attempt to help with cleaning or laundry. So by the time the following Friday arrived, she'd had plenty of time to prepare and dress and arrange things just so. She'd also had plenty of time to wonder about their sleeping arrangement and experience a few quivers of apprehension.

Kate descended the stairs in her new pale green dress, her hair carefully arranged and wearing the veil Charmaine had given her.

"You are beautiful," Marjorie told Kate when she caught sight of her. She'd been arranging the furniture in the parlor.

Kate blushed. No one had ever told her she was beautiful before.

"Noah left something on the kitchen table for you."

"What is it?"

"Go see."

On the table, she found a delicate bouquet

of dog's tooth violets and bloodroot, the stems neatly tied in a man's handkerchief. Kate's cheeks warmed even more because Noah had remembered her asking if she could carry flowers. She hadn't thought about it again until this very moment. What a surprising thing for him to do.

She picked up the bunch and raised it to her nose, imagining Noah climbing the foothills to gather the stems.

Outside, the sounds of a rig caught her attention. Having heard, as well, Marjorie came to her side. "Go on into the parlor. I'll greet your guests."

Luke and Annie Carpenter accompanied by Charmaine arrived first. "Noah has told me you're the local farrier," she said to Annie's dark-haired, blue-eyed husband. "He also says you own only the best rigs and the finest horses."

Luke grinned. "Then it must be so."

"Where is Rebecca this evening?"

"With her aunt Diana."

Dressed in a black suit and a plain white shirt with a string tie, Noah entered by the front door and stood to the side, unreadable and aloof as always, his hair covering part of one eye. His discomfort was obvious to Kate. She recognized that without his hat or gloves, he was feeling exposed. His sanctuary was being invaded by the very people he avoided. She smiled encouragingly, the bouquet held securely in her gloved hand.

Luke took a long stride toward Noah, shook his hand, then returned to join his wife.

Preacher and Mrs. Davidson arrived next. Tipper came in, followed by Fergie and the other hands. They'd all cleaned up for the occasion, slicked their hair and donned their best dungarees.

The preacher took control of the party and told people where to stand, then ushered Kate and Noah to their places and began the ceremony. He read scripture about a man and woman becoming one flesh and another about wives submitting to their husbands and husbands loving their wives as Christ loved the church. He then asked Noah to take her hand.

Noah held himself rigidly and she could tell it was with extreme reluctance that he extended his palm.

Kate glanced at the hand Noah was always

careful to conceal, noting the scar across his palm, and placed her fingers so it was hidden. She wished she had never listened to Estelle's talk of propriety and worn gloves. The fabric separating them seemed prophetic somehow, and she had a yearning to yank out of the glove and touch hands more intimately. Her neck and cheeks warmed as though she'd spoken her thoughts out loud.

There was a lamp lit on the wall behind the reverend and in it's golden glow she could see Noah's dark eyes and the discomfort in them. Having folks so close disturbed him, but he was doing this for her. And for Levi's baby. She gave him what she hoped was an encouraging smile.

When the reverend asked her to repeat the vows and asked her if she took Noah as her husband, she did so and replied yes without a qualm. Noah repeated the same vows and agreed to take her as his wife. Just one week before he had used those very same words when asking her to marry him. The words conjured up as much emotion at this moment as they had then.

When Preacher Davidson asked for the ring,

Noah released her hand and took a gold band from inside his black suit coat. "Give him your left hand."

"Oh." Caught unprepared, Kate held her hand out and was mortified to realize the ring Levi had given her was still on her finger.

Her face must have shown her distress, because Noah said quietly, so that only she could hear, "It's all right, Katherine."

He slipped the new ring on her finger and pushed it up beside the one his brother had given her.

"By the power granted me by the state of Colorado, I now pronounce you man and wife. You may kiss the bride."

Kate's heart pounded with alarm. She had kissed Noah's bearded cheek once and that's the closest they had come to a kiss. Surely if Noah hadn't wanted to kiss her, he'd have told the preacher to leave that part off. Wouldn't he? But then he probably hadn't thought of it any more than she had.

Someone in the gathering behind them cleared his throat. Noah looked into her eyes. *He'd taken her as his wife.* He leaned down and she raised her face to his. Expectantly.

He would kiss her cheek, she thought. Would those watching notice?

He'd taken her as his wife.

She closed her eyes, anticipating the graze on her cheek. When his lips touched hers and she felt the unanticipated warmth and pressure, as well as the slight tickle of beard and mustache, her eyes flew open in surprise.

He ended the kiss and straightened.

The witnesses applauded.

Kate's lips tingled. A smile started in her toes and spread through her body to her lips. Impulsively she captured Noah's hand and squeezed his fingers. He allowed her touch for a moment before withdrawing his hand.

Luke was the first to move forward and congratulate them.

Annie and Charmaine gave her hugs and Marjorie wished them both well. The hands ducked forward to greet them, then stood back awkwardly, as though they'd just as soon leave.

"Take seats wherever you like and we'll bring you cake and punch," Annie announced.

Noah took a chair at the end of the room, so Kate sat beside him. Mrs. Davidson was a cheerful plump woman with a dimpled smile. She chattered as she ate two slices of cake.

The few guests had brought gifts and Charmaine placed them in a stack in front of the newlyweds. "Open them."

Noah didn't budge, but gave her a nearly imperceptible nod. Nervous at being the center of attention, but excited, Kate scooted to the edge of her chair. She and Levi hadn't had a real wedding, and no one had given them a gift. Kate had never received so many gifts in her entire lifetime.

The preacher's wife had crocheted a set of four dainty white doilies. The hands had gone together and bought them a Seth Thomas clock to set on the mantel. Kate glanced at their faces with appreciation. Annie had sewn Noah a crisp white shirt and Kate a set of aprons. Charmaine gave them a china pitcher and bowl with roses painted on the sides. Marjorie and Tipper had bought a lamp—two glass bowls with floral decoration and a brass burner.

"You're all so kind," Kate said with heartfelt thanks. Somehow the gifts made the ceremony and their union seem more real than saying the words had. All of these people had witnessed and were acknowledging their marriage. "It was enough just to have you here. The gifts are…well, I don't know what to say."

"Thank you." It was the most Noah had said the whole time.

Marjorie and Annie washed the dishes. More good wishes went around, and eventually everyone said their goodbyes and left. Noah helped with horses and rigs and then stood on the porch watching the last visitor leave.

His emotions were in a turmoil. He'd wanted Kate to marry him so badly he could taste the need. He'd been so desperate to keep her here and to keep Levi's child with him that he'd been afraid the entire time that something would happen to stop their union.

She hadn't changed her mind. She'd seemed as sure as he, and that amazed him. But then he remembered his ploy on her need for security, the reason she'd come home with him in the first place. She needed a home and a place to raise her child. He was providing that. They'd discussed their arrangement and had agreed that this was for the best.

He ignored a tiny weed of guilt that now tried to grow and choke his satisfaction. He hadn't asked her to do anything wrong. He hadn't asked her to give up anything, and he didn't intend to make any demands on her. Having her here and having the baby in his home would be enough. He wanted to make her life easier, to provide for her and for his nephew.

Noah hung his suit coat on the porch rail and went out to the barn to overlook the stock. Jump and Harper were checking water pails and putting up two mares that were ready to foal. "We got this," Harper said to him. "You get on in to your new wife."

Noah surveyed the barn. Stepping outside, he studied the dark pasture and corrals. He glanced at the house and finally returned to gather his coat and enter.

Kate had filled the new lamp with oil and had it in the center of the table. She still wore the billowy veil with rows of tiny pearls. She was as beautiful as he'd ever seen her and her beauty had always awed him. She looked like a bride and her exquisite innocent charm made his chest hurt.

She glanced up. Her smile touched him in places he shouldn't be thinking about. "Have you ever seen anything equal?"

He shook his head slowly.

"I was wondering where we should put it. The parlor, I suppose."

"Wherever you like."

She carried the lamp to the other room, so he followed. She set it on a table and turned down the other lamp, so that the new one was the only one glowing.

"Something is bothering me," she said without facing him.

"What?"

"We didn't discuss…well. I decorated a room just to suit me, but that was before…well, before we decided to get married. It's not particularly frilly, but I don't know that it suits you."

"Doesn't have to suit me."

"I don't…" Her voice trailed away.

She was never at a loss for words, so he stared at her in puzzlement. "What?"

"Which room will we be sharing?"

Chapter Seven

Noah's blood rushed to his ears. His head felt light and the dark sense of shame that always pressed down on him closed in hard. What was she asking? What was she thinking? Did she think he expected her to share his bed? They hadn't discussed it because he hadn't thought it would be an issue.

"Nothing is going to change," he assured her quickly, his tone too harsh in its insistence. "You'll stay in your room and I'll stay in mine. As we've done. As we'll continue to do."

"Oh." She looked from him to the lamp, then surveyed the assortment of gifts still on the floor. He could see she was confused.

"We're going to live here together," he explained. "That's all."

"But we're going to be husband and wife."

"We *are* husband and wife."

She raised her chin and studied him. "Yes. But I was thinking…I guess I just assumed…"

She obviously didn't have words to explain her assumption and her cheeks turned scarlet with embarrassment. He disliked that she was uncomfortable—but he despised that she had felt *obligated.*

All he wanted now was to set her mind at ease and to smooth the tension between them. "It's not an issue, Katherine. Don't concern yourself."

He looked at her hand, at the pair of rings she wore. Levi had been the man she'd chosen for her husband. He'd placed his ring on her finger first. Noah's was merely a symbol of their agreement. It sealed her place here. But he didn't need to see the rings to be reminded that he wasn't her real husband.

He went to the kitchen and returned with a pail of water. "Ready?"

She extinguished the new light and, skirts rustling, climbed the stairs ahead of him. He carried the pail to her room. While she lit the lamp, he poured half the water into her pitcher. "Good night, Katherine."

She followed him to the door and closed it behind him. He stared at the wood a moment before turning and heading for his room.

Kate listened to his footsteps fade away.

She didn't know why she should feel this stabbing disappointment. Theirs wasn't a union born of passion. She should have known he intended to keep things the way they'd been, but she hadn't had much time to think about it.

When she had paused to reflect, she'd assumed they would share a room and a bed and the intimacies of husband and wife. The thought hadn't caused her alarm. Sex had been a main element during her brief marriage with Levi. He'd placed emphasis on the act, told her how important it was, and she'd learned to appreciate it.

Her enthusiasm dissipated like mist on a sunny day. This ache in her chest was the same she'd known back when she'd suspected that Levi never intended to return. It felt the same as when she'd realized he considered her of such little value. Disappointment. Rejection.

She pulled back the lace curtains and gazed down at the dark yard and stables. The tree outside her window had been pruned of all dead and singed limbs and now bore a hollow place through which she could see the stars. Seeing them reminded her of the trip to Copper Creek after Noah had come for her.

She'd promised to work, promised that she'd be useful. All her offers since she'd been here had been turned aside. Marjorie did the laundry and cleaning, Fergie did the cooking. Kate had done her own laundry and the last couple of weeks she'd been somewhat occupied with getting the bedrooms ready. What could she do to show Noah she was valuable?

She remembered Annie's story and how she hadn't been allowed to participate or to do things, either. Kate imagined she was feeling much the same way Annie had.

Kate wasn't one to feel sorry for herself. She was determined to shrug out of this and make herself useful. There were still a little over two months remaining until the baby came, until she found herself busy with an infant. She felt perfectly fine and there was no reason why she couldn't make a place for herself.

With a hollow ache in her chest, she removed the beautiful veil and hung it on the corner of her mirror, then tediously unfastened all the buttons of the prettiest dress she'd ever owned. Doubts rose up to torment her.

Somehow she had to prove herself worthy of being Noah's wife.

The following morning when she got downstairs, Noah had already left for the day. She found something to eat, then traveled to the meal house next door. It was a small house actually, painted and trimmed to match the big house, but was made up of an enormous kitchen and a dining hall only. She'd learned that Fergie lived in two rooms upstairs.

She found him dumping a bag of flour into a huge galvanized tub. "Morning," she greeted him. "It's a beautiful day today."

"Mornin', ma'am." Fergie was only a few inches taller than Kate. The thick mustache on his upper lip contrasted with the thin ring of hair around his balding scalp.

"What are you making?"

"Dough for bread."

"May I help you? I haven't any experience, but I want to learn."

"Lady of the house won't have much call for bakin' this many loaves of bread," he told her.

The familiar feeling of awkwardness came over her. Immediately she regretted coming out.

"Couldn't hurt if you learned how to make three or four, though," he added.

She beamed with pleasure. "Do you mean it? You'll teach me? Oh, thank you! I won't get in your way, I swear."

Fergie pulled over a stool so he could reach the top of a pine cupboard, where he shuffled through crates and jars and papers until he found what he was looking for.

"Always a good idea to start with a recipe when you don't know what you're doin'," he said, carrying the book to the waist-high table where he worked. "This here book has been to Texas an' back and I've figured out how to do a lot of things by readin' it and changin' ingredients and amounts to get me by." He flipped pages, found the one he wanted, then squinted up at her. "You kin read, cain't ya?"

She nodded. "Pretty well. I didn't get too far in school, but I got far enough to read and write and figure. I had a terribly mean teacher. His name was Mr. Himebaugh, and he used to whack us over the knuckles with his ruler if we misspelled a word or got our numbers wrong. Never made much sense to me, because after that, a person could barely write on their slate at all, what with their fingers all stiff and bruised."

Fergie made a *tsk*ing sound. "Sounds like a wicked fella. Also sounds like you know first-hand?"

She looked at the page he showed her and grimaced. "I'm afraid so."

"You follow the recipe there an' I'll watch ya while I do this."

She read the recipe, assembled the ingredients and heeded directions.

"Now knead it like I been a doin' here. Punch and roll and fold over."

Finally her dough resembled his and she punched and rolled vigorously. "Now I let it rise?"

"Yup. Cover it with a wet cloth and set the loaves over there where it's warm. You're pretty strong there, for such a fragile-lookin' thing."

"I worked at the laundry my whole life. Hauling water and scrubbing and wringing clothes takes a strong back and good arms and hands."

"I can see it does."

"Have you worked here on the Rockin' C for a long time?"

"Worked for Noah's pappy, I did."

"So you knew Levi."

"Yes'm. Always landin' hisself in a fix, that boy. He never stayed put longer'n a raindrop in a hot skillet. Got in so much trouble at school that his pappy gave a side o' beef to the school-teacher ever' year, just to pacify 'im. Scrapped at the saloon, too, Levi did. Black eyes'n bruises on that handsome face ever' Sunday mornin'. But he wasn't bad, that boy. Woulda gave you his last coin. Always laughin', always charmin', with a silver tongue that could talk you into anything."

"Yes, he was charming." Kate studied Fergie's precisely shaped loaves and found it easy to imagine Levi as an energetic young boy. His silver tongue had certainly talked her into a lot. She absently rubbed her belly.

"Only times I ever seen Noah laugh was when Levi was around. The lad would disappear for months at a time and be welcomed back at each return. This last time was the longest. I reckon we all feared somethin' was wrong."

Kate was trying to picture Noah laughing.

"On the other hand, Noah ain't been off this ranch more'n half a dozen times in as many years."

Her smile was sad. "Quite opposite, weren't they?"

"Yes'm. Levi so outspoken and engagin'. Noah all quiet and shut inside himself."

"Noah has his reasons."

"Yes'm."

By the time her loaves had risen, Fergie placed them in the ovens alongside his. Hers baked as golden and perfect as his, and she grinned from ear to ear when she saw them. "I can do this myself next time."

He wrapped her loaves and handed them to her.

She had just reached the back door when the sound of someone rapping at the front reached her. Since she'd been at the house, the front door was seldom used except just to go out to sit on the porch. Making her way through the house, she opened the door to find Estelle standing in the shade.

"Good morning, Estelle. Come in."

Estelle stepped inside and pinched off her gloves. "Thank you."

Her expression was no indication of what she was thinking. She always looked peeved to Kate. "What brings you out this way today?"

"I heard about the wedding."

Kate had wondered when and how she would hear the news and what she would do. She was Levi's mother, after all, and it made Kate uneasy to think Estelle would be angered, but she wasn't sorry they'd decided it best not to invite her. The day would have been spoiled.

"We decided very quickly," she replied. "I hope you're not upset with me and that you don't think I was hasty in making this choice. You're probably thinking there wasn't enough time between Levi's death and this new marriage, but Noah and I both thought it was a practical thing to do."

"As do I," Estelle said with a curt nod.

"Then…you're not angry with me? Or with Noah?"

"I think it's a very wise choice for you to secure the future of Levi's child. He will inherit his share of the ranch. By staying here, you're assuring him of his birthright."

"I feel even better about my decision when you put it like that."

"I brought you a gift." Estelle turned to the door and called to the driver. "Bring the package in, please."

A dark-haired man in a suit jacket carried a wrapped box inside. "Find Mr. Cutter now. Tell him I want a word with him, and then wait with the buggy."

The driver left.

Estelle turned back to her. "Go ahead," she coaxed. "Open it."

"Shouldn't I wait for Noah?"

She waved away the suggestion. "It's for you, not him."

"Oh. I assumed it was a wedding gift."

"Just a little something to bring culture to your life."

Kate resisted raising a brow and untied the bow. The wrapping gave way to a wooden box. Nestled inside were several carefully wrapped items. Kate removed one at a time to discover flowered cups and saucers, a matching teapot and several tins of tea and a shiny new brass kettle with a ceramic handle. "These are lovely. Thank you."

"You're welcome. Now I must speak with

Noah before I leave. Once again, I congratulate you on a wise choice."

Kate watched her march across the yard. The driver waited near the barn. Everything with Estelle was perfunctory and Kate had a hard time not letting the woman get on her nerves. She was going to be part of her life, however, so she'd better learn to deal with her.

Kate unpacked the gifts, carefully washed and dried and set them out on the empty sideboard in the dining room with the doilies Mrs. Davidson had crocheted. Stepping back, she admired the lovely china set. Would Noah notice? Perhaps it was better not to mention it. It would quite likely hurt his feelings that Estelle had deliberately brought a gift for Kate alone and not included him.

That evening she sliced the bread and served it with their meal from Fergie's kitchen. She watched Noah spread butter and eat half a slice before asking, "Do you like the bread?"

He glanced at the other half on his plate.

"I made it myself." She waited for his reaction.

"Why?"

"Because I wanted to learn. Fergie helped me, but next time I can do it alone."

"No need, really. He makes enough for all of us."

"I know he does, but I thought it would be good to learn how."

He went back to eating his meal and the subject was dropped.

A few minutes later she asked, "Did Estelle speak with you today?"

"Yes."

"She told me she wasn't angry about our marriage. Did she say the same to you?"

"She's not mad."

"I'm so glad. Do you think I should still be wearing black, now that we're newly married and all? I know it's respectful toward Levi, but it seems wrong in the light of a new marriage. What is right?"

"Don't know."

"I've been thinking about church and I was wondering…could you…I mean, will you consider attending church with me tomorrow? I know you don't normally go, and you told me your problem is with the people, but I thought if we went together it would show others that we're really married. And if you're with me, then Estelle won't be able to talk me into going home with her again, which I don't want to do. It was just a thought."

"No."

"Plain enough." She finished her meal and got up to pour them both coffee. She kept a pot on the stove and he always seemed to enjoy having fresh. She poured two cups and walked to set one in front of him. As she did so, she unthinkingly rested her hand on his shoulder.

Noah stiffened and sat up straight, practically recoiling from her touch.

She dropped her hand to her side and took a step back. "I'm sorry."

He looked away and waited until she moved to pick up his cup.

"Fergie sent a dish of pudding. Shall I get us each some?"

He shook his head. "I'll have it later."

After finishing his coffee, he stood, grabbed his hat and left the kitchen.

Kate watched him go, once again holding disappointment and rejection at tenuous bay.

That evening, as she intermittently read and walked from window to window looking out at the dark landscape, Kate made up her mind that she would go to church with the Bensons. If Estelle approached her, she would claim she'd promised to sit with Marjorie.

It didn't work quite that smoothly, however. Kate swore the look on Estelle's face when she saw her in her black dress was approval, but when Kate mentioned sitting with the Bensons, her haughty scowl returned. "That simply won't do. You're a Cutter, and Cutters don't sit back there with the hired help. Our pew is in the front."

Just then Annie and Luke entered, Rebecca on Luke's arm. Annie waved and joined them. "Good morning, Kate. Mrs. Cutter."

"Annie," Estelle replied. "Katherine's dress is perfect. I especially appreciate the princess pleats in her skirt and jacket that disguise her condition. Very tasteful."

"Thank you. I used the very same pattern for myself, in a blue sateen, but added braid trim and lace at the neck."

"I'm sure it's lovely, dear."

Annie turned a smile on Kate. "We'd love for

you to join us for dinner this afternoon. Will you please?"

Kate immediately jumped on the invitation. "I'd love to."

Apparently, Estelle didn't consider the Carpenters beneath her because she smiled and nodded. "That sounds lovely."

Kate suspected she hoped Annie would invite her, as well, but Annie only said, "Wonderful. You'll ride with us then, and Luke will take you home this evening."

Kate could hardly wait for the service to close and for her sentence in the Cutter pew to end. She practically shot up and ran toward the door while the organist played the closing strains of a hymn.

The Davidsons greeted her and she shook the preacher's hand.

"Glad to see you back, Mrs. Cutter," he said with a smile.

Kate greeted a few neighbors in the door yard as she waited for Luke and Annie, and then they found her.

Annie led the team herself. Luke rented buggies to churchgoers, so he had to wait until they were returned to the livery and then put up the horses. "We always hold dinner for him," Annie told her. "Even my mother's come to accept that my husband has a job where he gets dirty and occasionally smells like a horse."

To Kate's surprise, Sunday dinner wasn't at Annie's home, but at the Sweetwaters'. A huge porch surrounded the front and sides of the house. The enormous lawn was thick and green, and flowering trees and spring flowers grew in abundance. Annie introduced Kate to her older brother Burdell and his wife, Diana, who held their one-year-old daughter, Elizabeth. Their four-year-old son, Will, watched as his grandfather set up a croquet game.

Charmaine and her parents arrived, too, and Kate found herself in the midst of a lively family. Children ran and laughed while adults conversed and occasionally disagreed in a friendly fashion. Kate had never known anything similar and took it in with appreciation and surprise.

Luke arrived and sought out Annie. He took her hand and leaned forward to give her a quick kiss in greeting. Kate experienced a pang of envy at the devotion the two showed for one another.

Mildred Sweetwater and her kitchen helper served dinner. Conversation continued, and Eldon opened two bottles of wine. Annie and Kate declined when glasses were passed around.

The meal was delicious. Mildred's helper had gone home, so the women shared the task of cleaning up. Kate was delighted to be able to scrape and wash dishes and feel useful. She enjoyed listening to the women talk and occasionally she answered their questions about herself.

She joined a croquet game with Burdell, little Will, Rebecca and Charmaine. She'd never played before, so little Will explained the rules and the techniques in childishly convoluted sentences that Burdell interpreted. She watched to see how the others swung their mallets and hit the wooden balls.

When Rebecca swung, she hit her father in the shin. Luke fell to the ground, howling in mock pain. Kate laughed out loud. Rebecca ran over and kissed his knee, then showered his face with kisses.

Laughing, Luke tossed her in the air.

Watching him with his daughter created

in Kate a physical ache. She'd never known a father's attention or acceptance. Had never known a *parent's* attention or acceptance. She wanted so much more for her child that the need burned in her heart. She wanted what Annie's children had. What Diana and Burdell's children seemed to take for granted.

Would Noah play games with her child? Would he ever set aside his embarrassment about his appearance long enough to let anyone get close?

Tiring after the second game, she went to sit on the shaded porch with the women. Wayne arrived in a buggy and invited Charmaine for a drive. She waved to her parents and the couple rode away.

Kate exchanged a knowing look with Annie and knew they were both thinking of Charmaine's growing impatience for Wayne to propose.

The afternoon grew long and Luke offered to take Kate home. Rebecca begged to come along, so he made her a pallet on the tiny rear seat of the buggy. She fell asleep on the way.

It was dusk as they reached the Rockin' C, and the ranch seemed quiet and deserted. Noah walked from the barn to meet them and assisted Kate down.

"Thanks for bringing her home," he said with a nod to Luke, who remained on the seat. He wasn't wearing his gloves or hat, but Kate noticed he kept his head averted.

Luke touched the brim of his Stetson. "My pleasure. Have a nice evening now."

"Same to you."

Kate watched Luke go, then glanced at Noah. "Have you eaten?"

"Yes."

She picked up the hem of her black skirts and walked toward the house. "Well, goodnight, then."

Noah studied her back, wondered what she'd done all afternoon. He'd been surprised to see Luke Carpenter bring her home, though he shouldn't have been. Kate and Annie had become friends. Apparently she'd avoided dinner with Estelle. He wondered how that had come about and how Estelle had handled it.

He felt strangely bereft that she hadn't chattered about her day and all the things she'd seen and done, though he couldn't imagine why.

He'd always spent Sunday afternoons alone

at the ranch, a day of chores just like any other, but with fewer hands to do them. Strange, but since Katherine's arrival, the place seemed quieter when she was gone. The time passed more slowly.

Before her arrival he'd taken his evening meals alone. He'd liked it that way, preferred the solitude. Today, however, had been oppressively quiet. As he'd eaten, he'd been able to hear the tick of the Seth Thomas mantel clock all the way from the parlor.

The sound reminded him of Katherine. Of their wedding. Of the way she'd held his hand without cringing and allowed that affirming kiss with no outward sign of revulsion. Katherine was a strong woman, no doubt about it.

He'd secured her presence here by playing into her desire for a home for her child. She deserved to have friends and to see people. Whatever it took to make her happy.

Whatever it took to make her stay.

Noah had been asleep for only a few minutes when a tap startled him awake. He sat. Swung his feet to the floor and hurried to open the door.

Katherine stood in the silver moonlight that arrowed through the tall windows in the stairwell to the right of his room. She wore a white cotton nightgown and her hair lay in a thick braid across her shoulder and breast.

"What's wrong?"

"I just wanted you to know…I just had to say…."

"What?"

She raised her chin. "You may seek my bed any time you wish."

"What?" he asked again.

"You said you preferred our sleeping arrangements to stay the same, and that's fine. But I'm your wife now, and I wouldn't object if you came to my room for…well, I won't object if you come to my room."

Her sense of duty was admirable, however insulting. He'd be damned before he'd have a woman sleep with him out of a sense of duty— or out of *pity*. God forbid. His body didn't have any such reservations however and reacted immediately at the thought of going to her room and "seeking her bed." His arousal angered him all the more.

"I stay to myself," he said, hearing the bitterness in his voice. "I expect you to do the same."

"I meant no harm, Noah," she said softly. "I certainly didn't intend to bother or to offend you. Do excuse my lack of understanding. I—I won't bother you again." She turned and hurried away, her white gown trailing the floor behind her.

He didn't allow himself to step out into the hall to watch her enter her room. She wasn't his sort any more than any woman would ever be. He was what he was and nothing would ever change him.

He shut himself in his room. His heart pounded. His knees shook. Staring at the dark surroundings, his attention shifted to his bed and the rumpled sheets where he'd been lying.

He had no doubt that Katherine had meant what she'd said. If he walked down the hall right now and entered her room, she would accept him into her bed as her husband. The idea made his knees weak.

He'd stood in her room a multitude of times recently, supervising the work, rolling out the rug, assembling her bed. Thinking of her...

Remembering the feel of her in his arms as

he'd carried her from that room to his the night the tree had crashed through her window.

He knew exactly what her room looked like. Could guess how many steps from the door to where she lay at this moment.

She wouldn't even ask why he'd come. She wouldn't cringe or pull away. He'd seen her strength. He'd kissed her and she'd complied. She would comply again.

He resented his body for its blatant disregard for the impossible.

She wouldn't object. He could have her if he wished. He could remove her nightgown and discover the mysterious secrets of her lush body. He could kiss her, bury himself in her womanly scents and textures, satisfy this burning longing.…

He could have done the same at any time in his life if he'd been willing to humiliate himself by paying for the favor. If he didn't care that a woman had to look the other way when he removed his clothing. If he didn't care that he'd paid a price to have her ignore or pretend he wasn't disgusting.

Paid or pitying or obliged—all the same. All about shame.

He wished she'd never said the words. Wished she'd never told him she'd thought of it or that she wouldn't object. It meant she'd taken pity on him. It meant the security he'd bribed her with made her feel obligated. It meant he had to come in here every night from now until forever and imagine going to her room. His hopeless need was an embarrassment now.

He lay awake far too long and it seemed as though he'd barely slept when there was a knock at the door.

He stumbled out of bed and peered out into the hallway. Groggily, he realized a pail of water sat at his feet and he recognized Kate's footsteps on the stairs.

He'd brought warm water to her every other morning, but this day she'd delivered to him. Which meant she'd kindled and warmed the stove. The smell of coffee drifted along the hall. No one had seen to his needs since he was a child and her care was disconcerting. Noah washed and dressed, reflecting on the changes to his living conditions and his ingrained routine.

When he entered the kitchen, Katherine turned from the stove and carried a bowl of oatmeal to his place. Butter and syrup had been situated nearby and she set down a pitcher of milk before turning back.

He seated himself, prepared his oatmeal and picked up the spoon.

She carried buttered toast to him, then took her seat. Her oatmeal had already been flavored. It was an inconvenience for him to sit at the opposite end of the table, because if there was anything they needed to share, she was forced to hop up and down. Before her arrival, he'd never had anyone else present while he ate. Being watched made him uncomfortable.

As they ate, he couldn't help pondering if she was upset about the night before. He'd been abrupt.

But he'd learned in a little more than a month's time that she was quiet in the mornings. Once the sun was up, she chattered like a magpie, but upon awakening, she was unusually silent.

He found the trait endearing. And he felt privileged to know something so personal about her. Had Levi ever observed the fact?

For Noah's part, her silence wasn't much different from her chattiness, because he didn't feel compelled to respond to either. But this particular morning was different because of what had happened the night before. And because it was unusual—and in this case *unnerving* not knowing what she was thinking.

His gaze fell on the wilted flowers in a jar in the center of the table—the violets and bloodroots he'd picked for her. At the time he'd wished his roses had been blooming. She deserved roses.

He'd thought it a thousand times since he'd known her and he would think it thousands more: Levi should have loved her.

Chapter Eight

By Friday, Kate was proficient at baking bread. Not only had she made all the loaves that she and Noah consumed that week, but Fergie allowed her to help him bake for the hands. She took several loaves and stored them in the kitchen, then carried her soiled aprons to the laundry room.

It didn't take long to heat water, stir with the paddle, rinse and hang the clean items on the clothesline. Marjorie washed on Mondays, then ironed on Tuesdays. Kate had grown accustomed to the schedule and knew when she could do her own without getting in the way.

She admired her white aprons fluttering on the line before changing into a clean dry dress. After gathering her sewing, she added comfortable cushions to a chair on the front porch. Kate settled down with the tiny gowns she'd cut and pinned and began sewing seams and hems. The task gave her ample time to think. She wanted what Annie had, but so far she hadn't figured out how to go about getting it. She got things straight in her head, but then she ran up against the wall that was Noah.

An hour or so had passed when she recognized Estelle's buggy. Her visits were becoming a predictable routine and Kate wondered what it was she wanted to lecture about this time. The driver halted the conveyance several yards from the porch and helped Estelle down. Her starched black dress and crinolines rustled as she marched across the yard and climbed the stairs.

Immediately, Kate looked down at the skirts of the lightweight blue dress she'd changed into. Black was just so hot and stifling.

Estelle's disapproving gaze discovered her sin, but the woman didn't remark. Instead she seated herself on one of the porch chairs.

"Would you care for something to drink?" Kate asked.

"You should have help." Estelle gave an annoyed sniff. "Someone to fetch drinks when guests arrive."

"We have so much help now, there's barely anything for me to do," Kate replied with a wry smile. "I'm certainly capable of preparing tea or lemonade occasionally." She set down the tiny garment she'd been working on.

Estelle would expect her to use the teapot and cups she'd given her, so she made tea and carried the full pot and two cups out on a tray.

"I feel it's my duty to educate you in matters of manners," the woman told her. "Pour both cups, then ask if I'd like cream or sugar. After you've prepared mine, pass it to me. It's customary to provide tea cakes or cookies with afternoon tea. Next time I will bring recipes for the cook."

Kate's cheeks warmed. She knew how inept she must appear in Estelle's eyes. The woman meant well, but her lessons pointed out Kate's glaring inadequacies and made her feel more out of place than she already did. "Would you like cream or sugar?"

"Both please."

Kate reentered the house and finally found a small cup to pour a dollop of cream into.

She couldn't help comparing this strained time with Estelle to the friendliness and warmth of Annie's family. Estelle intensified all that was wrong with Kate's life.

"There are things a lady never discusses," Estelle said once she'd finished her tea. "But I am going to make an exception in this case, because of its importance to your position here and its significance regarding your vulnerability."

Kate set down her cup and folded her hands in her lap. Her curiosity was piqued. "What is it?"

"As shocking and inappropriate as it is to even have thoughts regarding the marriage act, I feel I must counsel you."

The subject couldn't have taken Kate aback more. Her skin warmed and she felt herself flush. "Please, Estelle. You needn't speak of this. I am not…a young innocent. I was, after all, married to your son."

Estelle held up a hand to silence her. "This is not a lecture or a warning against the ordeal. In any other situation and to any other young woman I would share clever advice for denying and discouraging unwanted overtures."

Confused, Kate made up her mind she would have to listen.

"In your case, Katherine, it's imperative that this marriage be consummated and that you bind yourself to the man by any means possible."

"What do you mean?"

"Has the marriage been consummated?"

Heat intensified in Kate's face. "No."

"You're not legally bound until that moment. Until then either partner can ask for an annulment and a judge can declare them never married."

Kate sat forward. "But we said our vows!" Distress sharpened her voice. "We signed the certificate!"

"Nonetheless, the act is necessary to fulfil the obligation. It's a vulgar act in any case, and I sympathize with your distaste at accommodating a devil such as the one you've married, but you have no choice. Fortunately for you, your condition will provide a good reason to discontinue contact for many months. Once you've gotten the deed out of the way, future overtures can be denied. Have I made myself clear?"

Somewhat dazed, Kate nodded.

"I understand your hesitancy, but once endured, it will be compensated for by your home and security."

There was still a possibility that Kate could be displaced. In the back of her mind she'd suspected as much. Was fear what had led her to Noah's room, prompted her to offer him access to her bed?

She didn't want to believe Noah would change his mind or turn her away. He'd never done anything to make her mistrust him. But neither had Levi. She'd learned the hard way that she had to look out for herself and not blindly trust. She had to seal this pact once and for all.

Estelle said goodbye and took her leave, and Kate washed and put away the teapot and cups in a haze of thought. Noah wasn't keen on the idea. He'd made it clear that he wanted her to keep to herself and that he intended to do the same. Should she mention this? Her prior attempt to talk about it had been met with anger.

Perhaps she should simply attempt to endear herself to him, and matters would work out on their own. She couldn't imagine that happening, however, not when the man didn't even allow her to sit beside him at dinner.

Kate walked out back to take her aprons from the line. Bringing the sun-warmed material to her nose, she inhaled fresh mountain air and sunshine. Kate gazed across the peaceful countryside toward the mountains, comparing Rock Ridge to the places where she'd grown up and worked. The ring of a hammer striking an anvil broke the silence and a cardinal bounced on a nearby limb before taking flight.

All she needed was one time. Once, and their legal joining would be concluded. She wanted to trust Noah to keep his word and his promises, but she'd trusted a man before and look where it had gotten her. She had to look out for herself and her child.

Estelle's words about Noah being distasteful chewed at her confidence in her ability to go through with it. How ugly was he? How difficult would it be to submit herself to a man she didn't find…attractive?

Levi's handsome features had been striking, he'd had a lean body and agile strength. He'd seduced her with skill and charm and left her dizzy.

After all, she wasn't really sure what Noah's features looked like. His beard and his habit of letting his hair fall over the side of his face prevented her from ever having a good look at him. Maybe she didn't want a good look. She'd seen his chest in the lamplight—maybe it got worse.

She felt guilty, somehow unfaithful for thinking it, but maybe she was better off not seeing him so she didn't have to deal with her reaction if it was negative.

By the time she'd finished her sewing and put things away, the meal house bell rang. She met Fergie in his kitchen, dished up plates for herself and Noah and carried them to the house.

A few minutes later Noah came in and they ate in silence.

He kept glancing at her. Finally he surprised her by asking, "Something wrong?"

"Actually, yes."

He laid down his fork. "What is it?"

"You don't need me to do laundry. You don't need me to cook. I have to sneak out to the meal house and help Fergie in order to have something to occupy my day. I know nothing of ranching or horses or cows, so my advice will never be of import. What is my place here?"

He glanced around, obviously struggling for an answer. "You're…you're…"

"What? What am I?"

"You're Levi's wife."

His words shot a needle of pain into her heart. Wishing he hadn't said that, she shook her head. "No. Not anymore. I'm your wife now."

The food Noah had eaten sat in his belly like rocks. She was his wife.

She was his wife and she wasn't happy. He was doing it all wrong, because he didn't know what the hell to do.

"There has to be something that's of value to you," she said softly.

"What do you want from me, Katherine?"

She pushed away her plate and laced her slender fingers on the tabletop. She looked lovely in her pretty blue dress. Looking at her hurt, because she was so pretty and so unattainable.

"Would you like a companion?" he asked.

Her forehead creased as she narrowed her gaze. "Pay someone to keep me company? Am I such a burden?"

"No." He'd bungled things again. "I aim to take care of you."

"The only thing I ask is that you let me belong."

If he knew how to make her feel better, he would. "How?"

"As long as our marriage is not consummated, the contract is not legal or binding."

The rocks in his stomach threatened to come up. The word "consummated" took on a life of its own, with inciting images and feelings he'd kept rigidly bridled. He swallowed. She'd offered to share her bed out of pity or a warped sense of duty. He'd turned her down. Would she leave now? Would she change her mind?

Bringing his brother's widow home and providing for her had been the honorable thing to do. Even marrying her had been noble. But *sleeping* with her?

He had to make her happy. He didn't know how to make her happy. He was out of his element. He wasn't Levi.

"And *if*," he managed to say, "then you would belong?"

"Then our marriage would be legal. We would be bound."

"We are bound."

"Not completely. Not in the eyes of the law."

He didn't know where the anger came from, but it swelled inside him and blurred his thinking. "Will what you're asking make you feel you've met your obligation?"

She was the one who looked away then.

He wanted to ask if it would make him more of a husband than his brother had been. Levi had done the deed, but he hadn't provided for her as Noah was doing. Clamping his lips tight on the words, he forced himself to remember her confusion and disappointment. She was doing the best she knew how, just as he was. And she felt insecure.

Nothing in his life had prepared him for intimacy with a woman. Levi was the only other person who'd ever had a good look at him without cringing or staring.

He'd never lost the shame or vulnerability of the day the doctor had come to the house and removed his bandages. His father's eyes had filled with tears and he'd looked away. Estelle had recoiled in horror. Only Levi had reached out to touch him. Only Levi had treated him as though he was the same person.

Shame and embarrassment was really a form of pride, Reverend Davidson had once told Noah when he was in his twenties during one of the man's visits to the ranch. If he could forego his pride, he could reveal himself.

Easy for Reverend Davidson to say, he'd thought. He didn't have to live with stares and whispers. He didn't have to look in the mirror and see a mouth that didn't move on one side. Once his beard had grown in thick, Noah had never shaved it off. And he didn't believe for a minute that shucking off pride would make a bit of difference in how he looked.

It had taken Katherine some time to formulate a reply, but when she delivered it, he knew she'd been planning her words. "I believe we both have an obligation now, Noah."

He couldn't eat another bite and pushed his plate away. There wasn't a choice now. If he denied her, the marriage wasn't sealed and they both knew it.

She stood and picked up her plate before pausing and sitting back down. "Noah?"

He was twice as big as she, but she struck terror in him. "What?"

"Is there some reason why...I mean is there a problem...from your accident that keeps you from...?"

He stood up so fast his chair flew backward and hit the floor with a whack. "Tonight, then."

Bringing a hand to her breast in surprise, she stared at him wide-eyed. "All right."

"All right." He punctuated the words with a nod, righted the chair and grabbed his hat on the way out the door.

There were still a good two hours of daylight left. He led the horse he'd been training out of the corral into the pasture, where he unhooked the lead. The animal kicked up its heels and galloped away, tail and mane flying. Noah would ride fences for a while, take one of the mares out for an easy ride.

Greta had a dark coat with a pale mane and thick forelock that hung between her eyes. He was partial to her nature and her looks, and had just bred her with an Irish draft.

He guided her along the fence line, his gaze instinctively checking the wire and posts without having to think much. His mind was completely absorbed with Katherine…and what he planned to do. It wasn't normal for a grown man to fret about something so natural. People did it all the time.

Levi had sweet-talked and bedded any number of women, then dismissed them as if they were cigar stubs. He'd often tried to drag Noah along for an evening, assuring him he'd loosen up if he had a poke.

Levi had won Katherine's heart, had married her and made love to her.

A twinge in Noah's chest pointed out how much the thought disturbed him. Sickened him. Terrified him.

He couldn't hope to compare. He had no idea what to really do. He was nothing like Levi. Was she expecting him to be? What *was* she expecting?

The sun finally set and Noah returned the horse and put it up for the night. Gathering soap, toweling and clean clothing, he set out for the stream. The water trickling down from the mountains was frigid, but he welcomed the check in his involuntary yet increasing arousal. He lathered his hair and beard and body, rinsed and climbed the bank, water streaming from his limbs and torso.

Dropping his head back, he gazed at the stars, tried to feel some of the same optimism that seemed such a natural part of Katherine. As reluctant as he was, there was a thrilling side to this that packed a wallop. He felt guilty for admitting to it, but, after all, he was a man. He would have to be dead to not want to make love to a lovely woman like Katherine.

The moonlight was a kind friend. He wouldn't let Katherine see him. With his ugliness hidden, he was just like any other. Noah dried himself and stroked a finger over the ridges on his chest. A lifetime of avoidance was not easily set aside.

He was not like any other man. His scars had become his identity.

He remembered the night Katherine's window had been smashed in by the tree and glass had showered the bed where she lay. After hearing the sound, he'd rushed to her room with terrifying visions of her cut and bleeding. The images had nearly stopped his heart. He'd immediately pictured cuts and gashes and blood. The unthinkable. Relief at finding her uninjured had come from his marrow.

Katherine was an enchantress. Hair the color of warm honey. Wide dark eyes that changed colors depending on the light and her clothing. Smooth cheeks and small dainty hands. She was fresh. Open. Guileless. She was everything he wasn't.

But her happiness at the Rockin' C seemed to depend on her sense of belonging and security, and she expected him to lock those in for her. No reason he couldn't. No reason he shouldn't. He picked up his dirty clothing and headed for the house.

The dressing gown Kate had selected was one Estelle had purchased from Annie's shop. It was pale blue sateen, with ivory lace at the neck and wrists, and ribbons that tied the front closed. Underneath, the matching sleeveless nightdress was the nicest thing she'd ever felt against her skin.

Kate had brushed her hair and rebraided it twice while waiting for Noah's footsteps in the hall. Did he mean to come to her room or did he expect her to go to his?

Waiting and wondering was nerve-racking. With Levi, she had always known his intent and he'd wasted no time in pursuing it. He'd been exciting and fun, with no inhibitions or qualms, and from him she'd learned that the physical act with a man was pleasurable.

She still had no idea what Estelle had gone on about, because it hadn't entered her mind to deny Levi once they were married.

Noah, on the other hand, was reluctant. If everything about him was contrary to what she knew, would the experience be an unpleasant one? She wanted to endear herself, to please him…show him he'd made a good choice in marrying her. But she didn't want to hate being intimate with him.

At the far end of the hall, a door closed. She hadn't heard him on the stairs; he wasn't wearing his boots. While she waited for another sound, her heart did a jig in her chest.

His rap made her jump.

"Come in."

He opened the door and stood in the opening. "Turn out the light."

She scurried to turn down the wick and extinguish the lamp.

He closed the door behind him with a solid click. "The shade."

She walked through a puddle of moonlight to lower the shade and plunge the room into complete darkness. Turning, she padded to stand at the foot of the bed, where she could barely make out the outline of his broad form. Noah.

"You're thinking this is awkward," she said. "But it's right. I know it is."

"Are you scared?"

She couldn't remember a time in her life when she hadn't been scared. "A little."

"I won't hurt you."

"I know that. Do you want me to take off my nightgown?"

It took him a moment to reply. "What would you like to do?"

She liked that he'd asked. "Well. I think I'd like you to kiss me."

"You…want me to kiss you?"

"Yes. Unless you don't want to. It was just a suggestion, but if you'd rather…"

He took a step forward and she felt the heat from his body through her clothing, though he wasn't touching her anywhere. Yet. The clean scent of soap emanated from him. He wrapped one strong arm around her back to gather her closer and bent his head to find her mouth.

Kate raised her face and they bumped noses before she sensed his mouth move over hers. When they touched hers, his lips were warm and firm. He kissed her tentatively and against her chin his beard was soft, his mustache a gentle tickle on her upper lip.

They were both a little uncertain, a little wary, but that didn't keep the kiss from being more pleasurable than Kate had anticipated. Quite naturally she leaned against him, her breasts and belly pressing against the muscle and sinew evident through their clothing.

Noah wasn't much taller than Levi, but he was a lot broader through the chest and shoulders. The arm around her back was firm and muscular. She'd known, because he'd carried her from her room to his, but she hadn't taken time to appreciate it then. Now she tentatively raised her palm to lay it on his shirt front, to feel the warmth, the beat of his heart. He was big and solid and reassuring.

The kiss ended and he leaned forward, nudging his nose into her hair, then lowered his mouth to her ear where his breath fluttered. Gooseflesh rose on her arms and shoulders, and her breasts grew taut. With one hand splayed against her back, Noah nuzzled the skin behind her ear and touched his lips to her neck.

Raising a tentative hand, she found his hair

surprisingly thick and soft, and ran her fingers through the cool, damp strands. She tucked a mass behind his ear as she'd so often seen him do, then trailed her fingertips around the shape.

He raised his face from her neck until his nose and lips barely touched her cheek. "You're not afraid of me?"

There was a touch of disbelief in his husky whisper.

"Do I need to be?"

"I don't think so. No."

She turned her face into his beard. He smelled like mountain air. "You sound uncertain."

"I'd never hurt you. Scaring you would be unintentional." His lips were inches from hers again.

This wasn't what scared her. This would ease her fears. But he couldn't understand. She tilted her chin upward.

This kiss was less hesitant than the last. In a kind of mutual exploration, both parted their lips. His thumb moved in a caress against her spine. The pleasure of his kiss an unexpected delight, she raised her other hand to his shoulder.

Noah wasn't sure who was leading whom in

this gratifyingly indulgent exploration. If she had any qualms about what they were doing, she hid them well. But then, she'd done this before and Levi had been experienced. He had to carve the humiliating thought out of his head and concentrate on the feelings.

Her body felt small and soft against his. The heady feminine scent of her hair and skin was new and enthralling, like nothing he'd imagined. He'd been in a state of arousal since he'd told her this would be the night, but being in her room, holding her in his arms and kissing her was almost more than he could bear.

He wanted her. Tightening his hold, he pulled her more closely against him and felt the swell of her firm belly. The reminder brought Levi to mind, but the crush of her soft breasts eased his brother from his thoughts. When he bracketed her ribs and took measure of her slender frame, his thumbs came up to rest on either side of her breasts.

She pulled away. Had his touch been too much? A stab of hot shame pricked his heart.

The sound of fabric rustled as she removed her silky dressing gown and dropped it in the darkness. Recognizing his first self-conscious instinct had been wrong, his heart stopped for several beats. Another rustle and he dimly made out the shapes as she pulled another garment over her head.

His throat had gone so dry, he couldn't swallow. He wasn't even sure he could breathe. Was she naked? His heart started beating again, this time like the chug of a locomotive. His blood thundered in his head and his scalp tingled. He would welcome the distraction of her chattiness right now before he made a fool of himself, but she wasn't talking.

She moved toward him, quite easily nestling herself against him where she'd been before, but this time when he reached for her, he encountered warm skin. He brushed her arm first, then moved both hands to her sleek back and ran his palms upward and back down, the back of his hand moving against her bumpy braid.

Mercy, she was silk and satin and heat and every delightful sensation his sanity could bear. Her skin was softer and smoother than anything he'd known.

She leaned into him and this time he knew the only thing between his chest and her breasts was his shirt. He groaned and dipped his head to her shoulder and reverently kissed her skin.

The position allowed him to dip his hands lower and cup her rounded bottom. Kneading her flesh, he pulled her closer and she flattened both palms on his chest.

With tactile pleasure, Noah stroked her derriere. This was too good to be happening. It took a moment for the fact that she had reached for the buttons of his shirt to register. When it did, he removed one hand to still her fingers. "What are you doing?"

"Taking off your shirt."

He'd known they would arrive at this point. She'd been brave enough to remove her clothing. But she was perfect. His body wasn't a work of beauty like hers.

It was dark, he assured himself. He'd planned it this way, waited, shut out all the light. She wouldn't see. After allowing her to unfasten the buttons, he shrugged out of the garment.

She backed away a step as though waiting.

He reached for his trousers and unfastened them, pushed them off and kicked them aside.

She moved away then, and he thought he'd done something wrong. But his eyes had adjusted enough that he could make out her silhouette in the darkness as she pulled back the covers and got into bed.

He stood there like an idiot, his blood pumping, his chest hurting.

"Noah?"

"What?"

"Are you coming to bed?"

He made his feet move then. Around the end of the bed. To the side. She couldn't see him. He was a man like any other, and he was her husband.

Not her first husband, that wretched voice in his head taunted.

Already he was inept and bungling things. He'd heard Levi talk about women's bodies and the things he'd done with females, but Noah hadn't any idea how to initiate such intimate acts. He thought everything so far had been incredible, but for once he didn't know what Katherine was thinking.

She was so perfect. Hair and lips and hands like an angel, skin that sent a man over the edge. His brain tortured him with thoughts of this sweet woman with Levi. She carried his child in her body.

"Noah?"

This would make her happy. Make her feel secure. His weight made the mattress dip and the bed frame groan. He lay and faced her, their knees touching.

"What would you like, Noah?" she asked.

"What do you mean?"

"I told you I'd like kisses," she answered. "Now tell me what you'd like."

As if the kisses hadn't been for him, as well, he thought. He wasn't going to admit he hadn't any idea what he liked. He was liking all of it too much. There was something he'd imagined, however. "Could you undo your braid?"

He could hear her smile in her voice when she said, "Of course." He sensed her motions. A minute later she found his hand between them and carried it to her hair where it spilled across the pillow. He wished then, more than anything, that he wasn't bound to the darkness. That he could drink her in with his eyes and appreciate her loveliness. At that moment he resented being cheated out of the pleasure.

Rising up, he kissed her. This time as they spontaneously embraced, he folded her close.

The bones of her shoulder seemed too fragile in his hand.

Katherine's palm met the skin of his chest and he froze. His entire being focused on her hand and the scars she was touching. He took his mouth from hers and caught her hand.

"What is it?" she asked. "Have I done something wrong?"

"No."

She placed her head against his chest. "Won't you let me touch you?"

Touch him. Years of conditioning fought the concept.

Her voice, so soft and gentle, carried the power to humble him when she asked, "What are you afraid of, Noah?"

Chapter Nine

What was he afraid of? That she'd run scream-ing into the night. That he'd lose this tentative bond he so desperately craved. That she'd be just like everyone who'd ever looked at him and turned away with revulsion in their eyes.

"How can we do this if I'm afraid of where to put my hands?" she asked. "Is there any-where…any place safe to touch you?"

There were few areas unscarred, the insides of his thighs—not that he'd suggest that— his feet, one calf, the right side of his torso. Working to keep from trembling, he carried her hand to his side and flattened it over his rib cage.

She stroked his skin and he shuddered. No one had touched him since he was thirteen years old. He was starving for this and frightened of it at the same time.

"I'm your wife."

Yes. The fact held him in awe.

"It's okay to touch me."

She didn't have to say it again. In the darkness he found the curve of her shoulder and grazed his touch downward until he held the weight of her breast in his palm. His throat tightened. She was exquisite. Her nipple hardened against his palm and he feathered his fingers back and forth across it to feel its nubby tip.

Katherine rolled to her back so he could treat the other in the same fashion. She raised a hand to the flesh of his back and pressed her palm flat. Distracted by her body's intriguing responses, he allowed the touch.

Noah bent over her and she met his lips in a kiss more urgent than any previous. The freedom she allowed made him bold enough to discover the swell of her belly and the curve of her hips. Silently cursing his pathetic aversion to light, he recognized his shame had robbed him of seeing something incredibly beautiful and unimaginably erotic. She was made for pleasure—visual and sensual.

She turned onto her side to face him and kissed him back in a melding of lips and tongues andbodies, pressing herself against him until his engorged penis lay cradled between her soft thighs.

She ran her palm over his chest then, her touch fueling the fire in his body at the same time it signaled his brain. He caught her hand and moved it to his ribs. Wedging her knee between his thighs, she once again stroked his chest. This time he didn't stop her.

He cupped her bottom and moved against her, and she felt so incredible he feared this time would be over before it had really started.

She eased back, taking him with her, and parted her thighs.

Noah supported his weight away from her stomach. "You sure this is all right?"

"I think so. If it hurts, I'll tell you."

He leaned on an arm that trembled and explored the secrets she offered, amazed at her yielding folds of softness. He found a slick ridge that, when he passed the pad of his fingers over, made her draw a quick breath. "Hurt?" he asked.

"Oh, no," she whispered.

He devoted his attention to eliciting a reaction from her.

"Kiss me."

Kissing her was his incredible pleasure. Touching her, a privilege that awed him. And when she tensed her body and dug her fingers into his shoulders, he intuitively positioned himself and entered her. She gave a little cry he didn't think was pain, and he captured the sound against his tongue.

She was heat and sensation and all-encompassing ecstasy, and he couldn't believe anything this good was happening to him. By what great hand of fate had he been placed on this earth at this moment and with this woman to experience such an incredible union? It was happening too fast and there was nothing he could do to stop it.

Though the room was pitch-black, he saw stars. With her head cradled in his hand, he shuddered against her, into her, and groaned with release. So as not to crush her, he moved beside her and she turned with him, her fingers laced in his hair.

His heart was still racing, but his mind cleared enough so that he asked, "You all right?"

Kate hadn't expected the rush of pleasure and emotion. She'd been prepared to carry out an act for the sake of her marriage. That she had enjoyed it was a delightful surprise. "I'm perfectly fine. Good, even."

Noah lay with his wrist draped over her hip, his fingertips caressing her spine in lazy circles. Her belly was pressed against his abdomen. She threaded her fingers through his thick, wavy hair over and over, and he made a sound of gratification deep in his throat. She dared to lower her hand and stroke his shoulder.

His fingers stilled their movement on her back for a moment, but he resumed the caress. There had been few places within her reach on his flesh where she hadn't encountered ridges. She wished she could see all of him in the light, know the extent of his self-consciousness and understand.

But perhaps she would be repulsed. Perhaps the sight was worse than the feel, worse than what she'd glimpsed that night in his room. Perhaps it was for the best he kept his scars hidden.

The baby rolled and a tiny limb battered her belly.

On her back, Noah's hand fell still.

The kick came again, harder this time.

"Is that the baby?"

"We must have wakened him," she answered. She took his hand, scooted back slightly and placed his palm over the place where her child was still moving.

An unmistakable lunge and roll indicated an active infant. Having someone with whom to share him was another joy she hadn't anticipated. Hot tears formed in her eyes at the intimacy of lying here with Noah and introducing him to her child.

For months she'd been afraid of the unknown future, the burden she carried alone and the uncertainty of her life. Tonight and for all the nights to come, she and her baby were secure.

She felt a twinge of guilt now that they'd shared this experience and Noah had been so incredibly kind and gentle. He'd never given her cause to doubt him or his word. But her baby's welfare came first. He'd never know the paltry existence that she'd experienced growing up. Her child would have a good home. A man to teach him. A share of the ranch.

"Thank you, Noah."

He'd grown still over the last moments and now said only, "For what?"

"For coming for me. For taking care of me. For providing a home for me and the baby."

He eased away and her skin felt chill as the air touched her. Standing, he moved to the end of the bed and she imagined him groping for his clothing.

"What are you doing?"

"You're welcome."

She sat up and reached for the sheet. "Noah?"

"Good night, Katherine."

The door opened and closed. Silence wrapped around her.

Kate clutched the sheet to her breasts, her body still tingling from his lovemaking. It had been good for her and she'd believed for him, as well. But he had told her he planned to stay to himself and expected her to do the same. There would be no change in sleeping arrangements.

He'd accommodated her request and that

was that. Perhaps he found her added girth offensive or the baby she carried an unpleasant obstacle. Perhaps he simply had no feelings for her. Why should he? She was a burden he hadn't asked for. A duty. Another responsibility when he already had plenty of them running the ranch.

She had hoped to endear herself to him. She splayed her hand across the sheet where it was still warm from his body and felt his absence like a physical ache. She could acquire greater value yet. Things took time. They'd only been married a week. There was plenty of time.

Katherine's thanks were a bitter taste in Noah's mouth through the night and the days that followed. He left the house early and didn't return until late.

One part of him wanted to mount a horse and ride into the wind, shouting. His first encounter with a woman had been nothing short of incredible. Well, short and incredible, he admitted.

The other side wanted to kick something, hit something or somebody, and rage. He'd known what he was doing when he'd offered her security to stay. He'd used it as a way to keep her here. And now that it had worked, he hated that his ability to provide and protect was the reason Katherine was here.

He wasn't Levi. He wasn't one of any number of charming handsome men who would be more suited to a woman like Katherine.

Katherine. Even her name was pretty. Katy. If he was another man he would call her Katy.

During the week that passed, he worked long hours and came to the house tired. Still, he couldn't keep his thoughts from her or his eyes away when they were together. On Saturday evening, he entered the house to cooking smells. He hung his hat and Katherine turned from the stove to give him a hesitant smile.

"What're you doing?" he asked.

"There was a dance in town, so the hands left early. I told Fergie to go on. I'm fixing your meal."

"I could have gotten my own meal."

The smile disappeared. "I'm sure you could have."

He didn't want to hurt her; he just needed to keep a safe distance between them. He'd never been this vulnerable before and he didn't like it.

"Wash up and have a seat. I've fried ham and potatoes. I also cooked beets for you because I know you like them."

He washed and sat at his place where she'd laid out silverware and a glass of buttermilk.

While she finished dinner preparations, he watched her with a hunger that consumed him. He had never seen it in the light, but he'd run his hands over the soft womanly body under that dress and apron. Her sweet smell and the taste of her mouth were ingrained into his memory and had consumed his every thought. The pleasures of her yielding body were incomparable.

Physically aroused, he lowered his gaze to the table. Her face was there in the wood grain, her sigh in his ear. He closed his eyes. She was there, too, her smile a secret in the darkness. His yearning for her consumed him.

Her footsteps neared and he looked up as she placed a plate of food in front of him. He remembered her touching his shoulder once as she'd served him and how he'd stiffened until she removed her hand. He remembered the night she'd touched him in the darkness and the sensation of her glorious hands on his skin.

The way Estelle treated him was normal. It was what he had learned to handle. Katherine's kind treatment brought upheaval to his senses and disrupted his way of life. Careful distance and not caring had always protected him. He had to concentrate on keeping his perspective to retain that safety, but it was difficult to do with her right here.

He reached for her wrist and surprised them both. Her bones were small and delicate beneath his hold.

She glanced down at his hand quickly, then into his eyes. He met her gaze and read curiosity—surprise and...*hope?*—in those dark hazel depths. Her face was perfection, gentle contours and ivory skin.

"Noah?"

She said his name often. He liked the sound of it more than he should have. He studied the bow of her upper lip, the tempting dewy pinkness, then tugged her wrist down so that she had to bend forward. As she did so, he captured her chin and jaw in one hand and turned her mouth to his for a kiss.

She didn't resist.

He slid his chair back and pulled her into his

lap. Noah held her head in place and kissed her more fervently than he'd planned. But then he hadn't planned to kiss her at all. He probably smelled like horses, but she didn't seem to mind. She tasted good and her bottom felt even better, pressed hard against his erection.

Their tongues melded in mutual longing and Noah caressed her breast through her dress. He'd planned to keep his distance. She wasn't obligated to him. He didn't want her pity or her favors.

God help him, he just wanted *her.* Wanted her with a ferocity and a hunger that scared him. What did he know of women, of keeping them happy? What did he know about being a husband? A lover?

Apparently enough, if the sound she made was any indication. A whimpering sort of sigh against his mouth that pumped fire through his veins as though lightning had struck him.

Dazed, he took her by the shoulders and held her away so he could breathe. So he could think. It was still light outside. At least an hour remained until dark.

"You're thinking it's too early." Her voice

came out breathy as though she'd just run all the way from Cedar Creek.

"Stop telling me what I'm thinking all the time."

She blinked. "I'm sorry."

"Don't say you're sorry. Don't move for a minute. Just sit there. Quiet."

She met his gaze in silent obedience.

Hating that he was so transparent, Noah released her. "Let's eat."

He caught her elbow as she stood somewhat shakily. He cleared his throat, scooted his chair back to the table and forced himself to eat. His belly was hungry but the rest of his body wanted more than food. "You going to church tomorrow?"

Sitting with her own plate, she nodded. "Do you want to join me?"

"No. But I'll heat you a bath. Take one myself."

"I'd appreciate washing my hair."

"Leave the dishes for Fergie tomorrow."

"What will he think?"

"That it's his job."

After they'd finished eating, he carried,

heated and poured water into the tin tub, then left her to bathe.

Three quarters of an hour later, he returned and used the water himself, then bailed it and stored the tub.

She hadn't resisted him at the dinner table earlier. She would never resist. The thought disgusted at the same time it enflamed. How pathetic was it to want a woman whose desire to please him was only to ensure her place?

He didn't bother with a shirt. It was dark enough now, and he strode to her room and knocked. He watched the crack beneath the door darken as her lamp was extinguished. *She'd been expecting him.* "Come in."

He closed the door behind him and took a few steps forward. In the darkness, he didn't locate her right off.

"It's okay that you don't want me to see." Her voice came from the bed. "I understand."

It was okay by him that she didn't want to see, as well. He found her sitting on the edge of the mattress when his knees touched hers. She'd left her hair down and he threaded his fingers through the barely damp tresses spread over her back and shoulders. She wore a satiny gown that allowed his rough touch to glide over her curves and capture her breasts.

He was fascinated with her body and silently cursed being blind to its lush secrets. He let his hands and fingers show him her beauty, acquaint him with the tantalizing swells and hollows.

She skimmed a palm over his bare skin above his trousers and his muscles jumped. Wrapping an arm around his waist, she pulled him close and pressed her cool cheek to his heated skin. Her breath fluttered the hairs at his belly and created a fire deep inside. When she kissed him there, he drew away and coaxed her to rise up and slide off the gown. He lifted her easily, moving her to the center of the bed.

Before coming back to where she lay, he shucked out of his trousers. Her mouth on his skin had disturbed him, but given him ideas... burning ideas...and permission.

Noah nuzzled her neck, kissed her mouth, then her shoulder, and lowered the caress to her chest. She captured his face with both hands.

"My beard bother you?"

"No. I wanted you to kiss me."

He discovered the texture of her tongue

against his, the silkiness of her inner lip, the satin skin of her neck and breasts. In her throaty responses he recognized that his pleasure in his new wife had only just begun.

The first weeks of June brought more sun and blooming roses. Early one morning mid-month, before the sun grew warm, Kate passed through the dining room in search of something to occupy her time. She had dusted and scrubbed and arranged and still, nervous energy prompted her to find tasks. She discovered a tarnished silver service in the marble-topped sideboard and polished the set until it gleamed. It would look handsome beside her tea set, so she arranged the pieces to her liking.

A movement on the other side of the lace curtains caught her attention and she stepped to the window. Noah moved among the rose-bushes, unaware of being watched. His hat lay near a patch of crimson nasturtium at the edge of the garden and his dark hair fell forward to his shoulders.

He straightened and glanced at the sky, and as he did so, his hair fell away from his face. The skin near his eye was puckered and pulled his lid up slightly. Kate stopped breathing at the sight of the ragged scars. She could only imagine what he'd suffered as a young man. Pain from injuries, yes, but the pain of rejection must have been equally as bad.

Through a crack in the dusty-smelling lace panels, she watched him bend and loosen dirt around the plants with a forked tool of some sort. Occasionally he used a pair of pruning shears to cut away a dying bloom. He disappeared for a few minutes and returned with a pail of water, which he poured around the base of one bush, then went for more water. He continued until each bush had been given a full pail of water.

The patience and care he used in tending his flowers was a contrast to the gruff uncompromising way he spoke to and dealt with people. He held the world—including her—at arm's length, but she believed she understood why.

He'd been tender with her when he'd come to her bed. Considerate. Accommodating. In their two brief encounters, she sensed he hadn't come to her because he'd wanted to, but out of a sense of duty and obligation. She had hoped to soften his heart toward her, but she had so few opportunities. When he entered the house of an evening, he held himself apart from her as he had since the beginning, not even allowing her to sit near him during dinner.

She watched as he finished his task, gathered the pail and tools and placed his hat on his head. With a last satisfied glance at his roses, Noah went on about his other work.

Pulling over an oak chair, Kate stood on it to remove the curtains from their rods to be washed. With effort, she pulled and pushed until the three windows were all open and the cool morning air drifted in. The scent of roses and damp earth wafted in, just as she'd imagined. Kate closed her eyes and took pleasure in her surroundings and her new life.

Turning to glance around the unused room, she imagined people seated at the long table, guests talking and laughing. How she would enjoy sharing a meal and a day or an evening with friends, showing them Noah's rose garden, and perhaps serving tea. Once she had the idea, she couldn't shake it.

She thought about an invitation the whole

time she carefully laundered the lace curtains and hung them outdoors to dry. She considered a menu as she polished woodwork and washed windows.

She searched and found a tablecloth for the table, but no napkins or china. That evening, she served their dinner in the dining room.

He glanced around. "Looks nice."

"The silver set is beautiful, isn't it?"

"Was my mother's. Never had a use for it."

"So many things in your home have a history, don't they? That's makes them all the more special. Do you mind that I got out the tea service?"

"No."

"I didn't find napkins or china. I was wondering if perhaps…well, if I could take in laundry to earn enough to buy a few things."

"Don't be ridiculous. You want things, go buy them."

"But…I haven't any money."

"Don't need any. Put whatever you want on my account."

"I'd feel better helping to pay."

"No. You won't take in laundry."

She studied him, but he cocked his head to

the side so she couldn't see his expression. "I was thinking about something else."

"What?"

"Wouldn't it be nice to invite a few people to dinner? It wouldn't have to be a Sunday. It could be of an evening."

"What for?"

"To visit, of course. To be sociable. Have friends."

"I'm not sociable. Everyone knows that."

She studied her plate. She knew, but she'd hoped he might consider a tiny change. Wouldn't benefit her to push him, however, so she'd best leave well enough alone.

"You want your friends to come of a daytime, go right ahead."

She looked up. "Do you mean it?"

"You're not a prisoner. Or a guest. This is your home. Do as you please. Just don't include me."

Quite naturally, a smile of anticipation and appreciation revealed her feelings. "Thank you, Noah. I'll invite company for next Monday, perhaps Tuesday. That will give me time to shop and bake and plan ahead. I'll invite Annie and Charmaine, of course. I could invite their mothers, too, and Diana.

"I'll go visit Annie first. I've been to tea at her home, and I want to find out just how I should do things. I've never done anything like this before, so I'm sure I'll be nervous. I want everything to be perfect."

Noah watched her get up and start to clear the table as she chattered. Why a body would deliberately want to do something that made her nervous, he couldn't figure, but just the idea had her delirious with anticipation, and he aimed to keep her happy.

"I have a blue-and-white dress I haven't worn yet. I've been saving it for something special." Her eyes sparkled in the lantern light when she turned a smile his way.

Her smiles had a way of infusing him with heat and eliciting a physical response he had no control over. His swift reaction drove his thoughts in another direction, so he let his gaze take in the swell of her breasts under her apron.

More than two weeks had passed since he'd been to her room. She seemed satisfied with their arrangement as it stood now, so he wouldn't push himself on her.

She went to the kitchen and returned with a flour sack wrapped around the handle of the coffeepot. She carried it to where he sat. As she filled his cup, he noticed the pair of rings she wore. Levi's ring on her finger was always a good reminder of his status, always helped him keep things in perspective. She'd been his brother's wife first. Noah was just the man who'd picked up the pieces after Levi had made a mess of things. She hadn't chosen Noah.

She'd needed him, but she hadn't chosen him. There was a world of difference.

Katherine turned down the wick on the lamp on the table, leaving only the wall lamp glowing. After doing so, she took a chair beside Noah. In the dimness, she turned to him.

Always accommodating, he thought. Always striving to please him and to meet his needs, no matter how inconvenient or strange.

"This isn't a necessary occasion," she said softly. "It's just a silly woman's fancy to invite friends. I don't want to take advantage of your generosity or make you uncomfortable. This is your home, Noah."

"It's your home, too. Whatever makes you happy is fine with me."

She reached for his hand where it lay on the table and he instinctively wanted to pull it away. Leaning toward him, she uncurled his fingers and cupped his palm against her cheek. "You care so much that I'm happy, do you?"

Her skin was warm velvet against his palm. He'd never known anything as sleek and perfect as this beautiful Katy. The ugliness of his scarred palm against her skin was an abomination and his stomach lurched at the defilement. He did pull his hand away then, refusing to see the disappointment in her eyes.

Yes, he wanted her happy. If she left now, his life would be empty. *But she was taking all the measures to make this work,* he thought with a prick of consciousness. She went out of her way to please him and he hadn't the slightest idea how to make her happy—except to provide for her and to make her life as comfortable as possible. He was keeping his distance to spare her. What else was there?

He knew most of her thoughts, since she never held anything inside. He should know what she would like. Guests to dinner, but that was out of the question. He thought back further. She liked to look at the stars. But she might get the wrong idea if he suggested stargazing. She loved flowers and the abundant countryside. She'd once asked him to show her the river.

"Tomorrow," he said.

She raised a dark puzzled gaze.

"Thought I'd go fishing in the morning."

She merely nodded.

"If you want to come, be ready at six. Pack something so you won't get hungry."

Her confused expression turned to smiles. "That sounds lovely! A picnic! It's something I've always wanted to do. It will be ever so much fun. Oh, thank you for thinking of it and inviting me."

All right, a picnic then. Had he just invited her on a picnic? He hadn't thought so, but somehow that's what had been arranged. His thoughts skidded to his men and to what they'd think about their boss taking a day off during the week to go on a picnic. Not a one would say anything, but he could well imagine their eyebrows shooting up.

Well, hell, it was his ranch and he paid them to work for him and if they didn't like it that he took a day off for the first time in…well, for the first time, they could eat dirt and he wouldn't care.

"We'll head out early," he said.

Looking up into his eyes, she smiled as though he'd given her the deed to a gold mine. That smile was worth more than gold. If he had a gold mine he'd give it to her right then and there. A picnic would have to do for now.

Chapter Ten

Noah hadn't intended to cause her more work, but the smell of frying chicken woke him while it was still dark, and he knew she was down there cooking. Eager to get away before the hands discovered his plans, he washed and dressed and buckled on his .45.

Katherine was bustling around the kitchen, washing pans and packing food when he entered the room.

"Everything's ready." Her cheerful greeting told him she'd been up for a while. "Fergie's cookbook came in handy again."

Noah headed for his back room. "Have to leave a note for Jump."

Once he'd scribbled a brief explanation and a list of chores, he carried the paper out and pushed it over a nail on the outside of the bunkhouse door, then gathered fishing poles and supplies and harnessed a horse to the buggy.

Katherine was waiting on the back porch, a shawl around her shoulders and a straw hat on her head.

He loaded the food basket and helped her up to the seat.

"Are we going to the river or the lake?" she asked once the buggy was in motion.

"There's a good spot where the river is wide and slow. I've caught sizable fish from the banks there."

As they rode, she chattered about the smell of wildflowers in the air and the last of the crescent moon overhead. Fine thing that he liked her voice, because he figured he'd hear a lot of it as time passed. The buggy disturbed the long grass of the riverbank where the crickets chirped a morning chorus. Beside him, Katherine inhaled. "Oh, my."

"What?"

"I can smell the river."

Noah set his other senses aside for a moment and concentrated on the scents. It did smell a little fishy as they neared the water. Eventually they reached their destination and he halted the horse.

"Wait 'til I come around." He climbed down his side and hurried to assist. The added bulk of the child she carried made her movements slower, but he barely noticed the additional weight as he lifted her to the ground.

It took a good half hour to start a fire, dig for worms, tie hooks and lines to their poles and get situated on an outcropping of flat white boulders that jutted from the bank. Noah folded two horse blankets together for her to sit on.

"Do you have to impale them?" Katherine's nose wrinkled in distaste as she watched him place a wriggling worm on a hook.

"Only way to get 'em to stay."

"But the worm's not dead yet. It's still wiggling."

"That's what attracts the fish."

Her expression was one of remorse. "Well, it seems cruel if you ask me."

"It's just the way things are."

She shrugged and after he'd thrown in her line, accepted the duty of holding the pole. "Doesn't it drown?"

"What?"

"The worm. Can it breathe under water?"

"Don't know." He baited his own line and threw it in the water.

"My pole keeps tugging," she said after several minutes.

"You have a fish."

"What?"

"Pull back and let me see. Sure enough. Look there."

Katherine laughed with delight and held the pole while Noah unhooked her fish.

"It's huge! Look at that! I caught one."

"A beauty, too," he replied, struggling to get the hook from the flopping fish's chin. Fishing was as natural as breathing to him. He'd spent many hours alone along this river. For Katherine it was a new experience and her enjoyment reminded him that not all of life was about work. "It's a trout."

"It is? Do trout taste good?"

"You're gonna find out."

She laughed again and her pleasure was worth all the sidelong looks he'd get from his men that afternoon.

"Guess sacrificing the worm was worth it, eh?" After releasing her catch into a basket set into the water, he baited her hook and tossed her line back in.

She'd caught three more by the time she became distracted by the rising sun. "Have you ever seen anything equal?" she asked in a breathless voice.

He'd been comparing her impressive catch to his two small sunfish, but at her exclamation, Noah turned his gaze to the palette of color streaking the sky, then to Katherine's face bathed in the golden glow of morning. "Never."

"I've always been up before sunrise to work, of course," she told him. "But there was always smoke and street noise and cooking smells and too much else going on to really take it all in. Out here, morning is the most important thing happening. Glorious, isn't it?"

Her expression was one of wonder and appreciation, a look he'd come to associate with her. She took nothing for granted, this woman he'd brought home and married. She looked at every day and each situation with a perspective foreign to his way of thinking.

Noah knew the sunrise was striking; he'd seen it a thousand times. But he turned his head now and saw the display of light and color with new eyes, looked at it from Katy's perspective. It was as glorious as she'd declared.

"Thank you for bringing me here." Her voice was breathy with emotion.

She deserved to catch all the fish. She deserved everything she'd ever dreamed for and never had. She was so appreciative and real. She deserved a husband as near perfect as she. Not a man like him. Hard. Scarred.

He'd tried hard not to hold a grudge against the Man Upstairs for what had happened to him. But the longer he knew Katy, the more difficult that grew. He wanted to be a man who could love her the way she needed. She spoke of Annie Carpenter often, as though Annie's life was an example she admired. It probably was. But Noah had always found it easier not to look at what other people had.

The sun rose bright and warm, and he admired her profile when she removed her hat and turned her face up to the sun as though absorbing its heat. For a man who preferred to hide in the shadows, her action reminded him of how natural and unaffected she was in all ways. He adjusted his hat brim over his eyes.

The basket of fish was overflowing when

he declared they had enough for supper. He'd brought a bar of soap and flour sack toweling, so they washed their hands in the river.

On the grass he spread the worn quilts Katherine had packed and she arranged their meal. He enjoyed watching her move about, fussing with this and that, settling herself on the padding.

Everything about her fascinated him. The curve of her cheek, the wisps of hair at her neck, her delicate scents, the rustle of under-clothing. He knew the pleasure of her body in the dark of night, but those times seemed sepa-rate and secret from this Katy of the daylight.

Even the baby she carried was a wonder and a mystery to him. He thought of the child often, imagined life as it would be when there was another little person to consider and care for.

"Only two more weeks until the Independence Day celebration and the church picnic in town," she said, diverting his thoughts. "Annie and Charmaine have told me all about the festivi-ties. The church ladies decorate a wagon for the parade. So do the different businesses and the bank. I can't wait. It will be my second picnic after this one. At night there are fireworks."

He made a noncommittal noise and took a piece of chicken.

"Have you ever gone?"

"When I was a boy." Too many people. Too many gawking pairs of eyes.

Kate glanced at him. "Of course, we don't have to go. We could have our own dinner at home."

He turned his gaze on her. "No. You should go."

"My place is with you."

An arrow of regret pierced him anew. Just because he'd married her didn't mean his situation had changed. "You know I won't go."

"I know."

"There's no reason you shouldn't, though. I want you to."

Her dark hazel eyes revealed an inner conflict. "If you mean it, I'll go."

He bit into the chicken breast. "Good chicken."

Her smile told him he'd said the right things.

As Noah ate, Kate noticed the jagged scars on his hands, remembered the feel of his palms and the ridges that covered most of his body.

It was difficult not to compare him to Levi. She missed having someone to laugh with.

Noah was withdrawn and curt, avoiding direct looks and most contact. Levi had been outgoing and spontaneous. He'd been openly affectionate and skillfully ardent in his pursuit of her.

She wasn't sure Noah even thought of her that way. He'd fulfilled the act because she'd asked him to and because he'd agreed it should be done. Spontaneity had not been part of it. Nor affection. Noah was a man of duty and honor. What more could she ask?

Levi had given Kate three things: a silver locket, her wedding ring and her baby. The only one she valued was her child.

The morning after her fishing trip, she opened the top drawer of her bureau and took out the locket. She wanted to buy fabric for napkins and a good set of plates for the luncheon she was planning, and she couldn't bring herself to charge the items to Noah's account. Food was one thing, these extravagances were another, and jewelry would probably bring her a few dollars in trade.

Kate had been delighted with the silver filigree necklace when Levi had given it to her, but now that she knew the gift was part of his coercion, she resented the object and the manner in which she'd received it.

It was hers. Levi had given it to her. She could do with it as she pleased. She tucked it into her pocket.

It took two shopping trips to gather everything she needed, but Newt was accommodating and drove the buggy to town for her each time. When Estelle made her regular visits to the ranch, Kate didn't mention what she was planning. The luncheon was her idea and the guests were her friends and she didn't want Estelle's advice or intervention.

By the following week, Kate had sewn napkins, baked tea cakes and cookies and arranged things just so. She was so nervous that morning, her hands shook as she put the finishing touches to the table. Marjorie had been a big help, supplying ideas and recipes, and then she ducked out to return home before Kate's guests arrived.

Kate changed into her new blue-and-white pin-striped dress and felt like a princess.

Annie, her mother Mildred, Charmaine, her mother Vera, and Diana all arrived in one buggy, Annie driving a splendid team of grays. Jump hurried out to help the ladies down before he unhitched the horses and hobbled them in a grove of trees to graze.

The women wore colorful day dresses, white gloves and feathered hats and traveled in a cloud of various perfumes. Kate admired their clothing, and Mildred confessed she'd made nearly all of her dress herself before asking Annie to do the finish work.

"It's beautiful, Mrs. Sweetwater," Kate told her sincerely.

"I never took a needle to anything except embroidery in my life until Annie chose to be a dressmaker. Now I can't help but find design a fascination." She tilted her head. "I still don't believe women of privilege should be employed, mind you," Mildred told her. "But I've seen how much Annie enjoys running her shop. And her daughter is well cared for. Annie is happy, that's all that matters."

"My mother has taken up painting," Annie told her. "You'll have to see her work."

Mildred blushed. "I'm not very good, really."

"Nonsense," her sister-in-law Vera contradicted, then looked to Kate to say, "She is incredibly talented."

Kate smiled. "Everything is ready if you ladies will please come in and be seated in the dining room."

The women admired Kate's decorating, her tea set and the silver service, then exclaimed over the chicken and vegetable soup she and Marjorie had prepared.

"I baked the bread," Kate told them proudly. "I make bread every week for Noah and myself."

At the mention of Noah, the ladies grew silent. None of them had expected to see him here today, but with the exception of Annie and Charmaine who'd been to the wedding, this was the first glimpse any of them had had of Noah's home.

"You're probably thinking that this house is plain compared to your home, Mrs. Sweetwater," Kate said. "Noah lived here alone for a lot of years. He had no call for fancy furnishings."

"Well, I'm sure you're just what the place needed," Diana said.

Kate wasn't so sure. Noah could have gone the rest of his life without change and been perfectly content. Sometimes she felt as though she was in the way or even an intruder.

Conversation turned to the Independence Day celebration and what the others would be bringing to the picnic.

After they'd finished lunch, Kate suggested they sit on the shaded front porch and have tea. Annie stayed inside to help her with the cups and tray.

"You seem a little quieter than usual," Annie said. "Is everything all right?"

"I have a lot to be thankful for," Kate told her. "I'm sure it's no surprise to you when I say that Noah married me because I was his brother's wife and had a baby on the way. He was concerned about the child."

"I'm sure he was concerned about you, too."

"Yes. And he was feeling obligated because Levi married me and then got himself shot."

Annie arranged the cups on the tray. "There's nothing wrong with living up to one's obligations."

"No, there isn't. It's just not very pleasant to *be* an obligation."

"I'm sure you mean more to him."

"I don't know. I…oh, I don't know."

"Go ahead, tell me."

"I don't feel important. Or needed. I'm another mouth to feed and someone to work around."

"I'm sure Noah doesn't see you like that."

"I don't know how he sees me. I've tried to make myself more valuable, to learn to do things and contribute. But Noah always tells me there's someone else to take care of tasks and that I don't need to bother myself."

"He's probably just trying to make your life easier."

"Maybe. But I feel like I'm in the way most of the time." The kettle whistled and Kate poured boiling water into the teapot. "I shouldn't be saying these things. I'm very grateful to Noah and he's a wonderful man."

"The first year of marriage is tough," Annie told her. "It's normal to have a lot of adjustments to make. And you're more emotional right now because of the baby."

"I suppose so."

Annie gave Kate's shoulders a friendly squeeze. "I know so. Now put on that pretty smile and let's have tea."

It was midafternoon before the ladies were

ready to leave. From the back porch, Kate rang the dinner bell. Jump appeared and hurried to hitch up the Carpenters's horses and bring the buggy to the door yard.

"We had a lovely time, dear," Vera told her. "You're a wonderful hostess."

"Thank you," Kate replied, and gave the women hugs.

Annie shook the reins over the horses's backs and the buggy moved away. Kate watched until it had traveled down the road and disappeared from sight. A sense of isolation swept over her.

Even though she had made friends, she felt lonelier than she ever had. Back in Boulder she'd never had time for friends or teas or picnics. She'd never owned a nice dress or a pair of gloves. Now she had those things, but something was still missing. Something important. At least then—as hard as working in the laundry had been—she'd had a sense of purpose, accomplishment and self-worth.

She decided to take Annie's advice to heart and told herself this was a difficult time of adjustment. She had the added emotional upheaval of her physical condition, as well as adjusting to a new life while tiptoeing around a man who didn't care for her.

But she had so much to be thankful for. She would count her blessings every day. Feeling sorry for herself was a waste of time. The problem was…she had plenty of time to waste.

The following week the entire community was geared up for the annual Independence Day parade and picnic. The hands did their chores early Friday morning and headed out.

With Noah's permission to use the supplies, Kate had baked a dozen loaves of bread and baskets of rolls as her contribution. Newt waited on the back porch and when she stepped out, he was ready and eager to carry out her things and load the buggy.

"Thank you for waiting," Kate said.

"The boss told me to. He also said you was to ride in the buggy, not on the wagon, and I was to drive careful-like and not bounce the missus around."

"He said all that?"

"Yes, ma'am, he did. An' he tol' all us last night to keep an eye on you, and if you got tired, someone was to bring you home straightaway."

"He is protective of this baby, isn't he?"

"I reckon so, ma'am."

As fate would have it, the day was warmer than all that had preceded it. The sun beat down with a vengeance. Kate stood on Main Street outside Miss Marples' Ice Cream Emporium with the Carpenters. Luke held a gleeful Rebecca on his shoulders and she clapped as the colorfully decorated wagons and buggies rolled past.

Kate couldn't help thinking about her baby, wondering if Noah would be a good father to the child, if her son or daughter would be loved and lavished upon as Luke's and Annie's daughter was.

At the very least, he would have a lovely home and enough to eat. He would grow up on the ranch and have an inheritance. That was the promise that had brought her here in the first place. The rest—anything more—would merely be icing on the cake.

As the day wore on, Kate was more tired than she wished to admit. She ate little at the picnic and eventually seated herself on a blanket in the shade. The heat was taking a toll on her.

Estelle approached, wearing her oppressive

black crinoline, and the fabric of her skirt crackled as she sat beside Kate. She snapped opened a fringed fan and wafted air beneath her chin. "The heat is positively stifling."

Kate nodded.

"Perhaps you should have stayed at home and not exposed yourself to the sun."

"I'm just a little tired."

"You don't look well, dear. Is that man working you too hard? You must come stay with me. I have help."

"No, he doesn't work me at all. I have to look for things to do. He has help, too."

"A chuckwagon cook is not domestic help. He hardly counts."

"There's Marjorie, too. She does laundry and helps clean."

"Nonetheless, it's far too harsh a life for a woman, especially one in your condition."

Kate's feet were swelling inside her shoes and perspiration trickled down her spine. She had the unkind urge to swat Estelle away as though she were a pesky fly. At that moment she just didn't have the stamina to deal with the woman.

Kate didn't think she could make it through

another several hours until the fireworks. Even though she'd been anticipating this day for weeks, its appeal had dimmed. She skimmed the crowd for a familiar face.

As she watched, Newt walked toward them with his distinctive bow-legged stride, a jar of lemonade in each hand. Kate smiled when she saw him coming and Estelle turned to see who she'd acknowledged. A frown crossed her features.

"Mizz Cutter, Mizz Cutter," he said, glancing from one to the other, then chuckling. "I sound like I'm repeatin' myself. Thought you'd like a spot of lemonade. It's real sweet and it's cold."

"Thank you, Newt." Kate took the jar. "Sit a moment, won't you?"

"Yes'm." He doffed his hat and knelt on the grass a few feet away.

The lemonade was indeed refreshingly cold and sweet. The best she'd ever tasted.

"If you don't mind me sayin' so, ma'am, you're lookin' a might weary."

"Positively wilted, you mean." She dabbed at her cheeks with a damp handkerchief.

"No offense, ma'am."

Estelle sniffed, got to her feet and left the

untouched jar of lemonade abandoned at the edge of the blanket.

Kate watched her go. "Might as well not let a perfectly good drink go to waste."

Newt agreed and drank half the liquid in one gulp. "The boss'll have my hide if I don't offer to take you back to the ranch."

As much as she hated missing any of the celebration she'd been looking forward to, she recognized the wisdom in his offer. "I believe I'll take you up on that ride, Mr. Warren. Would you mind finding Annie Carpenter to tell her I'm leaving, and then come back for me?"

"Right away." He shot up and disappeared into the gathering of townspeople. A few minutes later he returned with Annie at his side and she said goodbye.

Then Newt helped Kate to her feet, walked beside her and helped her into the buggy.

The road seemed dustier than usual, bumpier, and the air was hot and dry. They arrived at the Rockin' C and Noah, having seen their approach, met the buggy in the door yard.

"The missus is tired, boss. I brung her home just like you said."

"Thanks, Newt. Saddle a horse and ride back. I'll put up the buggy."

The young man headed for the barn.

Noah helped Kate to the ground. "Are you feelin' poorly, Katherine?"

"I confess my feet hurt and my back aches a little. I'd love to cool off and rest."

"Would you like a bath?"

"It's too hot to carry in the tub and heat water."

"Sit in the kitchen and I'll get the tub. The water doesn't need to be hot. Warm'll do."

"Cold would do."

He set about bringing the tub into the kitchen, carrying water and heating a kettle. When everything was set, he ran upstairs and returned with a dress and pile of underclothes. "Don't know anything about women's underpinnings, so I grabbed a fistful."

"They'll be fine, thank you."

"I'll be out on the front porch, making a place for you to rest when you're done."

She watched him go, grateful for someone to take charge and see to her comfort. Shedding her damp clothing and stepping into the water felt so good that tears came to her eyes. For a few minutes, she just sat and let the water soak into her parched skin and sooth her aching body. Occasionally she heard Noah's footsteps on the stairs. Propping her feet on the end of the tub, she could see how swollen they'd become. Her toes looked like little sausages. Finally she picked up the soap and sponge Noah had left for her use and washed.

She hated to leave the cooling water, but she stood and dried herself before stepping out onto toweling. She selected and donned drawers and a chemise, then a loose dress, and left her feet bare.

She padded through the parlor and discovered the front door open. On the porch, Noah had set up a narrow bed, complete with clean white sheets and the pillows from her own bed. He was just placing a crate with a pitcher of water nearby. She stared in surprise. "Noah! A bed on the porch?"

"It's a bunk from the bunkhouse. I beat the mattress and covered it good. This is the coolest spot of an afternoon. Shade from that tree there and from the porch overhang. You should be comfortable."

"Why, I'll feel positively *slothful* lying about like this."

"It's your job to take care of that baby. You'll be doing your job."

She looked him over then. His shirt was damp down the front, dark circles under his arms. He'd been working while all the hands and the townspeople took a day off. "You went to all this extra work on my account."

"It's my job to take care of you."

"Why don't you go use the bathwater and get yourself cooled off?"

"River's cooler."

"But the tub is right there."

"So it is. Holler if you need anything."

She watched him enter the house before lowering herself to the soft mattress and lying back.

Wind stirred the leaves in the trees and a cricket chirped somewhere nearby. Kate turned onto her side, made herself comfortable and let her muscles relax.

From her position, she could see a hawk circling over one of the pastures. The few clouds in the sky were thin and wispy.

Noah's consideration touched her. Kate's eyes

grew heavy as she thought about the small kindnesses he showed her. She drifted to sleep wondering what it would be like to be loved as well as cared for.

Chapter Eleven

When Kate woke, the sky was streaked with orange and red. Noah sat in one of the old rockers beside her, one foot absently keeping the chair in motion. He was wearing a faded blue shirt that looked soft, and the gun he normally wore wasn't present. His hair had been washed and combed back away from his face, revealing more of his features than she'd ever seen at once before.

She liked his forehead, strong and high. His brows were dark, but nicely shaped, though a white scar slashed the left one in two. The skin at the corner of his eye was puckered and the scar extended into his beard.

She'd grown to like the soft beard that covered the lower half of his face, simply because it was familiar and it characterized him. She

wondered what he would look like without it—
or if she wanted to know.

Their eyes met.

"Feel better?" he asked.

"I think so." She sat up. "I need to make a
trip."

Noah leaned forward and pushed her slippers across the floorboards toward her. "Want
help?"

"No."

He raised both palms. "Okay."

Kate stepped into the slippers, then walked
around the outside of the house to use the privy
and returned.

When she got back, Noah had sliced an apple
and made two sandwiches. "Hungry?"

"I could eat something."

She picked at her food, but he ate heartily.
Belatedly, she realized he was used to a big
meal before this time of day.

"Sorry if I spoiled your afternoon. You didn't
have to stick around while I slept."

"Didn't mind."

She imagined all the holidays he'd spent here
alone while the hands spent time with their

families or in town with friends. He was no stranger to a quiet afternoon.

"Did Levi go into town on holidays like this?" she asked.

He nodded. "He was a lively one. If there was a good time to be had, you could count on him to partake."

How well she knew that now.

"What about your father? Did he join in the festivities?"

Noah seemed to think about it. "Seems he stayed here a lot of the time, too."

"Maybe he stayed to keep you company."

"Maybe."

Kate glanced out across the countryside, appreciated the late sun gleaming from the aspens leaves on the mountains in the distance. "Do you ever want to go other places, see other things?"

He immediately shook his head. "I'd still be me. No matter where I went, I'd take the same situation along. There's no getting away from who I am."

"I guess we'd all like to get away from our situations at some time or another."

"Most people count on a situation to improve."

Kate drank the milk he'd brought for her. "Do you take after your mother or your father?" she asked, changing the subject.

"My father."

"He was a big man?"

He nodded.

"What did your mother look like?"

"Dark hair. Slim."

"Pretty?"

"I thought so."

"And she liked roses."

He nodded.

"Did you and Levi have a good childhood growing up here on the ranch?"

"For the most part. Worst was my ma dying. I was about four, but I remember her. My father married Estelle soon after and Levi was born."

"So he was only nine when you had your accident?"

"About that."

"Everything changed after that, did it?"

"Pretty much. Never went back to school. Stayed here and worked. Levi grew up, had friends, had interests other than horses."

"But you were close, the two of you."

He nodded. "He was full of life and so much

energy. Seemed like he was always on the move." Noah looked at his hands as he spoke. "he wasn't critical, easy to be around. Levi was the only person I ever spent much time around." He glanced up as though realizing how much he'd revealed and changed the subject. "You don't talk about your mother."

Guiltily, Kate realized she hadn't thought much about her, either. Since the day Noah had come for her, she hadn't looked back, except to be grateful she was out of there.

"What did the two of you do on holidays?"

"Nothing different. The laundry was rarely closed. Nobody stops wearing clothes, you know."

It was the most they'd ever just sat and talked. Kate was seeing a side of Noah he'd never revealed before. He seemed almost relaxed, more at ease with her and with the things they discussed.

"Tomorrow I'm going to send for the doctor," he said then, surprising her.

"Why?"

"Have a look at you. Name's Martin. Good doctor."

"Do you think that's necessary?" She got up

and moved to sit in the other rocker. "I'm not sick or anything. Just a little tired, and the heat got to me."

"You're not sick, no. Just want to know everything's okay."

"With the baby, you're talking?"

He nodded.

The baby. Everything was about and for the baby. Kate experienced a stab of guilt for feeling jealous about that. After all, she'd come here so the baby would be taken care of. "Whatever you say."

Crickets chirped and the sky had grown dark while they'd been talking. A cool night breeze drifted down from the mountains. "Do you want to go inside?"

"Not just yet. It's a pretty night."

Half an hour later in the distance, the sky was lit by exploding fireworks.

"Know you had your heart set on the celebration in town," he said after a few minutes.

Now that she thought about it, she'd enjoyed herself more with Noah tonight than she had at the parade or the picnic she'd so looked forward to. She'd especially liked the time they'd spent together talking. "I did look forward to it," she answered. "But this is nice. It's quiet and relaxing."

"You handle disappointment real well."

"What do you mean?"

"Make the best of everything, I mean."

"It's a waste of time to regret, don't you think?"

"You're never sorry about what happened with Levi?"

He'd never discussed this with her before. "It happened—nothing I can do about it now." She absently placed her hand on her protruding belly. "I can't take it back."

"Nothing you're sorry about? Wished it hadn't happened?"

She wondered what he was getting at. "Should I be sorry about something?"

"I'll never be Levi," he said.

"No, of course not."

"I'll never be Luke Carpenter, either."

She frowned in the darkness. "I know that."

"Has to be disappointin'. But you're not one to complain."

"I don't expect you to be someone else. What gave you the idea I'd be wishing that?"

He shook his head and she saw the movement in the moonlight that filtered down through a trellis.

Using the arms of the rocker, Kate pushed herself up and stepped to the stairs where she could see the heavens. "Look at all the stars. God has fireworks on display all the time, doesn't He?"

"I reckon."

"If I could wish on one of those stars and have anything I wanted, I don't know how much more I could ask for. Except maybe…"

"What?"

"Oh, I don't know." The dream of a family like Annie's had skittered through her head. A husband who loved her and needed her. But Noah had just told her he wasn't Luke, and she didn't want to make him think she wasn't grateful, because she was. "What would you wish for?"

He didn't answer. Finally she turned around. "Noah?"

"There aren't any wishes like that."

Practical as always, the man, dashing the wind from her fanciful sails with a few words.

"No, of course not." She turned back to pick up the dishes.

Noah stopped her with a hand on her wrist. "What were you going to say when you stopped? What would you wish for?"

She looked at his hand and in the darkness it looked like any other. "A real family," she replied. "That's all."

Noah took his hand away. He couldn't give her a real family. He could take care of her and provide for her, but he couldn't be who she wished for.

If he had any wish in the world it would be to go back and change what had happened to him to make him a solitary man in hiding. He imagined standing in front of her without scars or self-consciousness. Often in his dreams he walked down Main Street greeting people, going about his business, and no one gawked or whispered because he was Noah-without-scars. It was the most liberating dream. Waking always left him bereft to be in his real body.

She picked up the dishes. "Thanks for today. I feel much better."

He watched her open the screen door and enter the house.

* * *

The doctor had pronounced Katherine fit and healthy and suggested she rest with her feet up several times a day to keep the swelling down.

His assessment eased Noah's fears and he asked Marjorie to check on Katherine often over the next few weeks. The hot July days were the hardest on her, but she seemed to have more energy in the cool of the evening.

Toward the end of the month Noah worked closer to the house. He worried whenever she was alone and was glad to see Annie visit occasionally. Even Estelle's regular visits to the house assured him that Katherine wasn't alone.

One oppressively muggy afternoon, he was chasing calves up out of a ravine toward the herd when the sky darkened and thunder rumbled in the distance. His first thought was to get the calves to their mothers before heading back to make sure the horses were in the corrals.

Lightning split the sky and with the resulting crack of thunder, a warning went off in his head. *Katy.* She would be terrified.

Chasing the calves up the bank, he got them started toward the herd and kicked his heels into his dun's flanks. Rain poured from the sky, pelting his hat, soaking his clothing. He didn't take time to reach for his slicker, just bent low over the horse's neck and rode hard.

Everyone would be looking after the horses. Marjorie would probably head home. He doubted anyone but himself knew of Katherine's fear.

Each jagged streak of lightning, every clap of thunder, made his own heart race because of how he knew it affected her.

The house and yard came into view through the downpour. The sky was dark and ominous, and lights shone from the kitchen windows.

Noah rode his horse right up to the porch, jumped down and slapped it on the rump so that it ran toward the barn.

His boots hit the floorboards and water dripped from his hat. He shucked both inside the kitchen door. No one was in the room and a fire was banked behind the isinglass window of the stove. "Katherine?"

He hung his .45. "Katy?"

She wasn't in the parlor or on the front porch, so he took the stairs in his stocking feet. Neither was she in her room. "Katy!"

"Noah?" Her voice came from his room.

He found her huddled in the center of his bed, the covers wrapped around her. Her hazel eyes were wide and her face pale. "Noah."

"Katy." He stretched out beside her and pulled her trembling body close. "It's okay. You're safe."

"I know. I knew I'd be safe here."

"Did you know I'd come?"

She shook her head against his chest. "You're soaking wet."

He pulled away long enough to shrug out of his shirt and denims and then crawled under the now damp covers where she was fully clothed. She felt good in his arms. He loved the silken brush of her hair on his skin, and she smelled like vanilla. "I smell like horses."

"No, you smell fine to me."

He hugged her instinctively.

"I'm glad you came. I'm sorry I'm such a baby."

"It's okay. Why did you come in here?"

"I don't know. You brought me here last time I was scared and I felt safe. I just feel safe here. I guess."

He liked that she felt safe in his room. That

she felt safe with him. Rain pelted the roof with a steady sound. Here inside they were cocooned and sheltered. Katherine's trembling had eased as they talked. She turned onto her side, facing away from him, and he molded himself along her soft, warm body.

Lying close to her was a pleasure he would never take for granted, and he felt guilty for the excuse of a thunderstorm to do so.

When her breathing grew deep and even he knew she slept. He allowed himself the secret pleasure of touching her hair, caressing strands and learning the silken texture. He rose up on one elbow and enjoyed her peaceful expression.

He was drawn to touch her and ran a finger across her perfect cheek, skimmed the delicate turn of her jaw. She was so exquisite, it almost hurt to gaze upon her like this.

Had Levi ever watched her sleep? Had he held her while storms raged outside? Had his brother ever considered more than his momentary physical pleasure when he'd looked at her?

He couldn't forget that she carried Levi's baby. The child would always be a reminder of the man they had both loved. Noah's gaze traveled unerringly to her hand curled upon the pillow, seeking the reminder that she had loved his brother.

What he saw made his ears ring and his heart pound.

She wore only one ring: his.

Kate woke to sun in her eyes and heat at her back. She squinted and peered at the window, then oriented herself. Noah's room. It was late afternoon. The storm had passed and the sun was low in the sky. Noah lay behind her.

Extricating herself, she sat. He slept, the sheet midchest, his shoulders and arms exposed. He was broad and muscled, his skin only half as tanned as his face and neck. The scars marring him were testament to the pain he'd suffered all those years ago. Many were ragged and V-shaped, some long and ridged, others small gouge marks.

Kate recognized the suffering he'd endured, understood his self-consciousness and knew why he hid himself. She'd fully anticipated being repulsed at actually seeing the marks on his body, but she felt only sorrow for the boy he'd been and regret for the way he'd turned away from people.

Her perusal moved to his face. He'd let her see him more and more of late, but she'd never been this close when his hair wasn't falling forward. He was fortunate he hadn't lost his eye, she thought. She observed the way his beard grew and the glint of red in it from the sun. Looking closely, she could see there was an area near his mouth where the hair wasn't filled in as thick, and he had a small scar at the corner of his bottom lip.

She had the strongest urge to kiss it.

Warmth pooled inside her at the thought of kissing him. She'd liked it before, and he'd been so very gentle and tender.

Following her impulse, she leaned forward and pressed a kiss against his mouth.

Noah's eyelids opened.

Feeling foolish, she met his gaze. His attention shot to the window, then back to her face. She realized too late that she'd violated his protective guard by looking at him while he was unaware. Because she knew how strongly he felt about her seeing him, it had been unfair.

"I guess we both slept," she said, sitting up and facing the window. Her clothing was damp and rumpled.

Behind her, she felt the bed move as he got up. A drawer opened and sounds indicated he was dressing.

"Thank you for coming home."

He didn't answer, so she looked over her shoulder.

He was buttoning his shirt and he met her eyes.

"Thank you, Noah."

He nodded in response, knelt to the pair of denims on the floor and pulled his pocket watch from a pocket. After flipping open the cover, he said, "Near time for dinner."

"I'll change in my room and be down in a little bit."

They ate together in companionable silence that evening. Sometimes Kate thought things between them were changing, but then at the next moment it was proved that nothing had. She was just foolish enough to let herself imagine things, and she'd like to think that Noah was growing to care for her—for Kate. If his concern over her well-being was only for the child she carried, she didn't want to face it.

She must have slept too much that afternoon, because she felt restless that evening. Her back hurt, and she had a hard time sitting still or focusing her attention on her sewing. She went through a stack of recipes Vera Renlow had given her, baked a spice cake and iced it. Knowing Fergie would be in the work kitchen preparing for the next day, she cut an enormous slice and carried it out to him.

By the time she returned and did up the dishes, she had to lie down. About a half hour later, Noah knocked on her door. "You sleeping?"

"No. Come in."

"Had cake and coffee," he said from just inside the door. "Best cake I ever had."

"Really?"

"Wouldn't say it if it wasn't so."

She attempted a smile. "No, you wouldn't."

"Are you feeling poorly?"

"My back hurts something fierce." Tears welled in her eyes before she could stop them. "I'm just not myself."

"Anything I can do?" He walked farther into the room, concern etching his features.

"Not unless you have a magic lamp."

"I can rub your back."

"That would be nice. I don't think I can sit up."

He came to her bed and seated himself behind her. "Don't have to sit."

He used the heels of his hands to massage and was careful not to press too hard or to stay in any one place overlong. He worked from her neck down her spine before giving his attention to both shoulders.

Kate closed her eyes and lost herself in the comforting, relaxing sensations. "You're hands *are* magic. I've never felt anything equal," she told him on a sigh.

After nearly half an hour he said, "I could make you tea."

"It doesn't feel right having you do for me," she answered. "I'm supposed to be making myself useful."

"You're supposed to be taking care of yourself and the baby," he argued.

"Very well. I'd love a cup of tea."

He brought it to her several minutes later. "Sleep well."

"Good night, Noah."

After she'd sipped half the tea, she got up and changed into her nightdress and climbed wearily into bed. She had slept for only a couple of hours when her aching back woke her again. She used the bedpan rather than make the trip out of doors and walked the floor, now at the brink of how much pain she could endure. She hadn't imagined anything like this when she'd thought about the baby coming. She thought of waking Noah, but this could take a long time and it was foolish to bother him simply because she didn't want to be alone. He worked hard and had to get up early. She would wait until it was time to send for the doctor.

She was still pacing when she felt a warm gush of fluid run down her legs. The pain in her back intensified and wrapped to the front, gripping her abdomen.

Kate saw stars for a moment. Terrified and in shock, she gasped, held her breath until the pain subsided and then awkwardly changed her nightgown. Pain gripped her again and she doubled over, then, after it passed, made her way to the doorway. "Noah! Noah!"

She heard something fall, then his door opened and he hurried toward her, his hair mussed, his chest bare. "What's wrong?"

She went back to her bed and lay down as he hurried in.

"What is it?"

"The baby's coming."

Noah lit a lamp.

Pain gripped her then.

He took her hand and she squeezed it for a moment.

"I'll send Newt for the doctor," he said gruffly.

She nodded.

He ran from the room and returned minutes later, wearing his shirt. He used towels to wipe up the fluid on the floor, then pulled the chair up close and seated himself. "I sent Jump for Marjorie, too."

"Okay."

"It's going to be all right."

"Yes. I didn't know it was going to hurt this bad."

His eyes darkened with sympathy. "I'm sorry."

"Maybe I'm foolish, but I never knew. I don't know anything about this or what to do or how to take care of a baby. I'm not ready for this, Noah."

"You don't have a choice. The baby will come

whether you're ready or not. It's going to be all right."

"Is it?"

"You'll learn how to take care of him. We'll both learn. Don't upset yourself thinking about that now."

Marjorie arrived first and Noah had never been so glad to see anyone. She gathered sheets and towels and boiled water, then instructed Noah to help her slide additional padding underneath Katherine.

He sat with his wife and encouraged her until the doctor came and told him to wait downstairs.

Tipper had come with Marjorie and he'd made coffee while he'd waited. "You may as well sleep, boss. It's liable to be a long night."

"I can't sleep."

"My rifle needs cleanin'—how about yours?"

They took apart rifles and then their .45s and cleaned and oiled them. Noah went for his shotgun next. By daybreak they'd gone into the bunkhouse, brought out every hand's shooter and replaced it clean.

Noah scrubbed the oil from his hands at the pump, then returned to the kitchen.

Marjorie had come down and was preparing a tray of food.

Noah glanced at the fixings. "Is that for Katherine?"

"No, it's for Doc Martin. He's missin' his breakfast."

"How is she?"

"She's tired, but she's doing fine."

"Is everything all right?"

"She's fine. Doc says a first baby just takes a while, is all."

"Should I come see her?"

"I'll come get you when the time comes or if she asks for you."

Noah followed her to the foot of the stairs and listened. All he heard was the click of a door and low voices talking.

Tipper put on his hat. "I'm gonna see to chores, boss."

"Thanks for stayin'."

"Sure." Tipper headed out the door.

Noah was torn between keeping busy with chores and remaining close by. He went out and forked hay down from the loft, then returned. The hands had all gathered next door for breakfast, but he didn't feel like eating.

A sound caught his attention and he ran to the foot of the stairs. Katherine was in obvious pain and distress, her cries echoing down the hallway. Noah's scalp prickled. Bile rose in his stomach. He sat on a stair, elbows on knees, head forward, and gripped his hair in both fists. He wanted to escape, but he couldn't bear to leave her.

Chapter Twelve

An eternity passed while his heart pounded and sweat gathered and pooled down his sides and back.

The sudden silence was louder than the cries that had come before. What was going on? Why hadn't he heard anything for minutes? Was something wrong? He got up and stood on the bottom stair.

Finally a door opened and footsteps sounded in the hallway. Marjorie appeared, looking hot and weary. "You can come up now."

"Is something wrong?"

"Everything's fine. The baby's just perfect."

"Katherine's all right?"

"Come see for yourself."

He bounded up and followed her to Katherine's room. Just inside the door on the floor was a ball of sheets, which Marjorie quickly picked up and carried away.

Doc sat in the chair beside Katherine's bed.

Katherine lay propped against her pillows, her hair damp and wild, her face flushed, but smiling. In her arms she held a blanket-wrapped bundle. "Come see her."

Her? His nephew was a girl? He took a few awkward steps forward.

"Isn't she beautiful? She has so much hair and a pretty little mouth."

Noah studied the wrinkled infant. Her eyes were scrunched shut and her head seemed odd-shaped. He would never have used the word beautiful to describe her, but he didn't place much store by looks. She was tiny but appeared healthy enough.

Katherine looked tired and the skin around her eyes was mottled with red.

"She's okay?" he said to the doctor.

"Baby's fit as a fiddle," he replied. "Both of 'em need some rest now."

He'd been inquiring about Katherine, but was distracted by the baby opening her mouth and making a mewling noise. Her tiny hand moved jerkily and Katherine gently cupped it.

"I'll be headin' out now," Doc said. "I'll come back in a day or so to see how you're doing. Any problems before that, send for me."

Noah told Katherine he'd be right back and followed the doctor out and down the stairs.

"It took so long, Doc. Is she…is Katherine all right?"

"She's fine, Noah. She's tired and rightly so. That was a lot of work. Looks like you could use some sleep yourself. That's what I plan to do when I get home."

"How much do I owe you?"

"Never know how to charge for helpin' birth a baby. Woman does all the work—I'm there for advice and emergencies."

"Took near all day. Day's wages seems fair to me."

"That sounds generous enough." He had a cup of coffee while Noah went back to his room and returned with silver coins.

"Thanks for coming so quickly. And staying. Is there anything I need to know or something I should do now?"

"Just get acquainted with your new family. I'll wager that girl child up there will have you wrapped around her little finger within the year."

Noah rang the dinner bell and when Jump answered the call, Noah asked him to fetch the doctor's rig.

After seeing the doctor off, he returned to the kitchen and found Marjorie preparing a tray. "I've heated soup for her. Sliced bread and poured milk."

"I'll take it up. You go on home and rest."

"Are you sure?"

He nodded. "Thanks for helping."

Katherine's eyes were closed when he entered the room, but she heard him and opened them.

"Here's some soup for you. You should eat."

"I don't want to lay her down in that cradle," she told him. "It looks so big now that I see how tiny she is."

Noah looked at the cradle. It looked baby size to him.

She turned those liquid eyes on him. "Will you hold her? She can feel your heartbeat and your warmth and know she's not alone."

Noah sat the tray on the bed beside her, then nervously took the minute bundle she trustingly handed him. The infant was light as air, barely weighing more than the flannel that wrapped her. The wonder overcame him and he stared in awe. Slowly he backed up to the overstuffed chair and sat.

Kate lit into her soup. "A girl, Noah. I never imagined. We always talked about her like she was going to be a boy." She paused as a question came to her. "Will she still inherit a share of the ranch? Even though she's a female?"

"Of course," he answered quickly.

His assurance was all she needed. "I was thinking in the back of my mind that I'd name him after your and Levi's father. It seems silly and you're probably thinking I should have been more prepared, but now I don't know what I'm going to call her."

Noah was taking stock of the new life in his arms, her feathery dark hair, the barely discernable lashes and brows, the way she held her tiny fists up by her face. He looked at every perfect fingernail in awe. "She's incredible."

"Have you ever been around a brand-new baby?"

"Not a human one."

"Me, neither. Doc said mothering comes natural to most women, but I can think of a couple who make that statement seem untrue. What if I'm not a good mother?"

He looked up finally. "Course you'll be a good mother. Look at all you've done to make sure she has a good home."

"What if I don't have the right feelings?"

"You worry about that when you didn't want her to be alone in that big empty cradle? Eat your dinner so you can rest."

She listened to him and ate. Finished, she set the tray away. "What are we going to name her?"

We? He looked from the baby to Katherine. "You asking me?"

"Yes, of course. You're her uncle, but you're going to be so much more to her. We're married, so you're her father now."

Noah's throat tightened up. All along he'd thought of teaching a boy to ride and work horses. What would he have to offer this girl child? The ranch. She would grow up to inherit the Rockin' C. He looked at the baby in a whole new light.

"What was your mother's name?" Katherine asked.

"She's Levi's baby. Estelle would have a conniption if we named her after my mother."

"Do you care?"

"Not particularly, but it doesn't seem fair to Levi somehow. What's your mother's name?"

She shook her head resolutely.

Noah came over and perched on the edge of the bed. They stared at the baby, then at each other. Katherine's eyes crinkled at the corners and a broad smile brightened her weary face. "I know," she whispered.

"What?"

"Rose."

Noah looked at the infant. Rose. A perfectly pretty and feminine name. His attention lifted to Katherine.

She looked infinitely pleased with herself. "Your mother loved roses and so do you. I think it's perfect."

"And she is perfect," Noah said. Like her mother. Rose was fitting of a beautiful woman. "I like it."

"So do I."

He handed Rose into her mother's arms, watched Katherine as she looked at her baby and touched her cheek with one finger. His heart was full. Here in this room he had more than he'd ever dreamed would be his. If he died tonight, he'd go to the promised land a happy man.

He had a family.

Rose was a greedy eater. It seemed to Katherine that she nursed every time she turned around. During those first days Kate was content to hold her, rock her, bathe her and sing her lullabies.

Each night Noah came to her room and held the baby before he went to bed. He finally convinced Katherine to lay her in the cradle and let her get used to sleeping by herself.

"Has anyone told Estelle yet?" she finally asked him.

"She'd be here if she knew. I thought you needed some time."

"Bless you for that."

"I suppose we should send word," he said.

"I suppose so."

They shared a look of regret. "I'll send someone in the morning."

Before noon the following day, Estelle had arrived with two bags and ensconced herself in one of the other bedrooms. "You should have sent for me. I'd have been here to help you."

"There wasn't time." Kate felt only the merest twinge of regret for the lie.

Estelle picked up the baby from her cradle and held her close. Her eyes filled and tears traced down her powdered cheeks. "She looks just like her father did as a newborn," she declared. "She has his face shape and his ears. Her hair is darker though." She glanced at Kate's hair with a frown as though it was her fault the baby didn't have her father's hair. "She is Levi's child through and through. I've been thinking of names, and I think she should have a strong name. Nothing too pretty, so she won't be too full of herself."

"Her name is Rose," Kate said.

Estelle looked up and blinked. "Rose?"

She nodded. "Noah and I agreed that it suited her. She's as fair and pure as a rose, don't you agree?"

"If you're certain you can't be persuaded to select something with a little more substance."

"Very certain. She's our little Rose."

Though the day was warm, Estelle reached into a nearby basket for a flannel blanket and wrapped it around the baby's legs. "You must keep her out of drafts for the first month or two."

"There's no draft, Estelle. It's August."

"She arrived a little too early, didn't she? Were you taking proper care of yourself?"

"Doc said she wasn't early."

"I'll show you how to bathe and dress her properly." Estelle took over and tended to the baby all afternoon, except for bringing her to Katherine to nurse.

Estelle stayed that week and the next, and her presence disrupted Kate's time with her baby, as well as Noah's visits. He didn't come to her room while Estelle was there.

The first time she gave Rose a bath, she warmed water, poured it into a basin and tested the temperature half a dozen times. The infant squalled until her face turned red.

"Please don't carry on so, baby," she said, afraid her nervousness was being projected onto the child and trying to keep her voice calm. "I'll have you clean in just a few minutes."

The infant's cries brought Estelle rushing to the kitchen.

"Is the water scalding her?"

"No!" Kate said quickly. "The water's fine."

"Baby's skin is far more sensitive than an adult's, you know."

"The water is not too hot."

"It's harmful to bathe a newborn too often. Their skin is too fragile."

"Marjorie said it would be all right to bathe her."

"What does Marjorie know?" Estelle pushed up beside Kate and reached for the squirming infant. "She is just a tiny thing, Katherine— you must take every precaution."

Kate backed away, unwillingly relinquishing her task. She stood by as Estelle finished bathing Rose and wrapped her in the soft toweling Kate had laid out.

Kate handed her a soft flannel wrapper she'd sewn, but Estelle pushed it aside.

"I brought gowns which were Levi's. I saved them all these years, and now at last I can see another child wear them."

Kate stood back and watched Estelle dress Rose in the garments she'd brought, trying to remember the loss this woman had suffered and doing her best to be tolerant. She dumped the water from the tub and rinsed it while Estelle took the baby to the other room to rock her.

That evening as they finished a quiet meal, Noah glanced at the baby who had started to fuss in the cradle which stood along the far kitchen wall.

Kate stood to go to her, but Estelle jumped up and took over the duty of changing her flannel.

"She's hungry," she told Kate in an accusatory tone, as though she didn't already know.

Kate took the baby from her, rejoicing in the fact that she was the only one who could provide the child's nourishment. She suspected Estelle would have been eager to take that job from her, as well. But their private time was characteristically brief, because the woman always managed a way to usurp Kate's rightful duties.

The days ran together in much the same fashion, with Kate growing more and more frustrated, and feeling like she was the outsider in the house. Her emotions were in a spin, and she often had to bite back tears or angry words.

With the woman fussing over the baby, Katherine did however find time to bathe and to do her laundry and bake bread. She felt good getting back into her routine.

One evening with Estelle upstairs in her room, Kate took Rose from her cradle and slipped down the stairs to the front porch. The bed Noah had set up was still there, and she had shaken out the spread earlier in the day. She settled on the mattress with Rose beside her and breathed in the fresh night air. Rose stirred and Kate stroked her downy hair.

The screen door creaked and Kate's heart sank. Estelle had discovered them.

But instead of Estelle's voice, Noah said, "Enjoying the air?"

Kate leaned up on one elbow. "It's such a pretty night. Have you come to join us?"

"If you don't mind."

"No. Do you want to hold her?"

He took the baby and sat in a rocker nearby.

She sat up and watched him rock the baby in the moonlight.

He glanced up. "Is Estelle a help to you?"

Kate said nothing for a moment. Finally she replied, "She loves Rose."

"I'd like to think that she's making things easier for you."

"She does do a lot for Rose." Kate wanted to cry then, for no reason, really, except that she couldn't say how she truly felt. Estelle made her feel inadequate and jealous. Kate resented her taking over her mothering duties, and it troubled her that she'd seen so little of Noah. Her throat ached with the loss.

"She's Rose's grandmother," he said.

"Yes."

"I'm respectful of that."

"As am I," she agreed.

He exhaled as though he was frustrated. "I'm not accustomed to your silence. You're not saying what you're thinking, and it doesn't feel right. I'm in the dark and I'm not liking it."

His uncustomary speech surprised her. "I'm sure she means well, and as you say she's Rose's grandmother."

"She worn out her welcome?"

Kate wasn't sure how to reply.

"You're tryin' my patience, woman. She's a help or a hindrance—which is it?"

"I don't really need any help."

"Damn near had to drag you behind my horse to get you to say it."

"She's your stepmother, Noah, Levi's mother, and I don't have any right to—"

"She'll be leaving in the morning then."

Her sense of relief was overwhelming. She almost cried from the feeling of a weight being lifted from her chest. With Estelle gone, things could move forward and Kate would have one less tension to deal with.

She enjoyed watching Noah hold Rose, enjoyed his expressions of awe and amusement, and she wished she could see his face now. Tomorrow would be the first day of their life together as a family.

Early the following morning, Noah rapped on the door to the room where Estelle was staying.

The woman opened the door and immediately turned her gaze aside.

"I'll have a buggy ready for you after breakfast. Be ready."

"What are you talking about? I'll send for my driver when I'm ready to go."

He turned and strode down the hall. "You're ready to go now."

She leaned out the doorway. "Katherine needs

my help. You can't prevent me from seeing Levi's daughter."

"You can see her any time you want. You just can't live here."

"You're a crude, boorish man, Noah Cutter! Your father would never have allowed you to treat me in this manner!"

"No, he only let you treat me badly," he replied as he hit the first step and started down. Behind him, she cast stinging barbs he ignored.

Newt was the first hand he ran across after that encounter. "In about twenty minutes go up and fetch Mrs. Cutter's bags. She'll be going home today."

Newt looked puzzled for a moment, but then his expression eased. "Oh! The elder Mrs. Cutter is leaving."

"Yep. You just happen to be the first hand I saw to ask to take her home."

"Sure, boss. I got a thick hide."

"I'll see to it Fergie saves you the best slabs of beef and the biggest pieces of pie for a week."

Newt grinned and went about his chores.

Noah stayed near the house to make sure Estelle left as planned. Sure enough she marched from the house, shrugged away from

Newt's assistance and climbed into the buggy. Newt planted his hat on his head and led the team away.

Later that morning, Noah spotted Katherine in the side yard, carrying a basket. She wore a sling he assumed held the baby. She was hanging underclothing on the clothesline.

"Should you be doing that?"

Startled, she turned and shaded her eyes with a hand to look up at him. "My laundry?"

"Marjorie could have done it."

"I like to do my own. It's what I know how to do, remember? And you won't let me help with the rest of the wash." She pointed out back of the house. "I've been wondering why we have such a small garden."

"Enough to feed us over the summer."

"But what about canning for the winter months? Putting up preserves and the like? I've heard other women talk about it."

"We trade beef and pork for goods already canned and preserved. Gives the other town wives something to barter."

"Oh. I see. Well, maybe next year we could have a bigger garden and I could learn how."

"No need wasting the effort." He glanced at the row of white drawers and petticoats, ribbons fluttering in the breeze, then down at the chemise in her hand. "Estelle's gone."

"Yes. Thank you."

"Thought she was a help, but I reckon not."

"No."

"You need more help with the baby, you come ask."

"I won't."

"Don't be too stubborn to ask."

"Okay."

He turned and headed for the corral.

A baby grew a lot in a month. By September, Rose had filled out and gained weight. She ate more at one feeding and slept for longer periods of time, though she was awake more often, as well.

Kate had visits from Annie and Charmaine. They brought gifts for Rose and exclaimed over her hair and eyes and admired her pretty gowns. Even the hands carved blocks and wooden horses and presented them to her.

Estelle visited twice a week like clockwork.

She brought clothing and toys and always asked to hold Rose.

Noah, too, paid a lot of attention to the baby. He took her out on the porch every evening and rocked her. Sometimes Kate joined them, other times she left them alone.

This evening Kate perched on the bunk Noah had left outdoors for her.

"Her head doesn't look so funny anymore," he commented.

She shot him a frown. "Her head never looked funny."

"Her eyes are a might bluer than yours."

"They are now, but Annie said they could change as she gets older."

"I don't think they will."

Kate loved watching him with her daughter. More and more she realized that Levi wouldn't have been the father Rose needed. Coming here, marrying Noah, had been the best thing she'd ever done for her child. And for herself.

She adored Rose and appreciated time to enjoy her and care for her, but she wanted to be more important to Noah, as well. She wanted him to need her and she needed to feel valued.

She wanted a real marriage and a real family in all ways.

She thought about it the rest of the evening, while she made Noah coffee, as she fed Rose and put her to bed, while she changed her clothing and brushed her hair.

She lay awake for an hour or more, listening to the night sounds through her open window, working down the oppressive sense that she wanted more. Sometimes she had an aching need to sob and felt guilty for having no good reason to do so.

In the distance a coyote howled its mournful cry. Kate got up and parted the curtains, looking out on the night. She had married Noah out of desperation. She didn't like admitting it to herself. But it didn't have to stay this way. They didn't have to have a marriage in name only. She had enjoyed their brief physical encounters. There was no reason they couldn't bring companionship and pleasure to each other.

No reason she should settle for less than what she wanted.

Kate checked on Rose, touching her warm cheek in a loving caress. Leaving her bedroom door open, she tiptoed out into the hall. The closer she got to Noah's room, the faster her heart beat, until she stopped and composed herself.

His door was open a few inches, but she tapped lightly on the wood. Then again. No response.

Slowly she pushed open the door. "Noah?"

Moonlight streamed across his rumpled bed. It was empty. She glanced around the room in confusion. She'd anticipated finding him asleep.

Kate gathered the hem of her nightdress and padded down the stairs. The front door was open, so she pushed open the screen and stepped out. Out here the sound of the crickets was intensified.

Noah lay on his back on the bunk, his hands stacked under his head. She tiptoed closer to see if he was sleeping.

He wasn't, because he saw her out of the corner of his eye and turned his head.

"What are you doing out here?" she asked.

"Couldn't sleep. I like to come out here 'cause it's cool." He sat up. "Is Rose all right?"

"She's fine. I didn't mean to disturb you." She

pushed him back down with her palm flattened against his chest.

He reached for her bare forearm and wrapped his fingers around it. His touched burned her skin. "You should probably go back in."

"Why?"

"All this…isn't easy for me."

"I'm sorry to have made things more difficult for you."

"It's not you."

"I want to improve your life, Noah. I'd like to feel I'm not a burden."

"You're not a burden."

"But your life was easier before I came."

He didn't reply, so she knew she was right. She sat at his hip. He still hadn't released her arm and the fact was encouraging.

The night air touched her through her thin gown, grazed her arms, making her feel naked. Gooseflesh rose on her skin and her breasts tingled. A shiver of delicious expectation slivered up her spine.

"You can't be cold," he said.

"No."

She remembered how much she liked kissing

him, how good he made her feel. She leaned forward and pressed her lips to his.

Noah inhaled sharply, as though caught off guard.

She molded her mouth over his and framed his face with her free hand.

Both of his arms wrapped around her then, pulling her down and holding her close. It was natural to fit herself along his body and lie against him. He groaned and kissed her more deeply, opened his mouth and sought her tongue.

Kate got lost in the pleasure, kissed him until her head grew light and her body heavy. She pressed herself against him and he adjusted their bodies so that she was lying fully atop him, acutely aware of his arousal.

Their kisses grew more insistent and Noah stroked her back and her bottom through the thin cotton, tugging the fabric upward until he touched her bare skin, and then he groaned.

Through the haze of passion, Kate dimly became aware of a sound. She lifted her head and listened past Noah's harsh breathing. A thin cry caught her attention. "It's Rose." She raised her body away from him and took his hand. "Come with me."

He got up and followed her into the dark house, locking the door behind them and hurrying up the stairs.

In her room, Kate went directly to Rose's cradle, changed her flannel and carried her to the bed. "Lie with us."

She settled onto the pillows and opened her gown for Rose to nurse. Noah stretched out beside her and caressed Rose's tiny foot.

Kate couldn't resist touching Noah. She ran a finger over his lower lip, brushed his soft beard and toyed with a lock of hair. He leaned over to kiss her.

They parted and turned their attention to Rose until she finished eating. Once she was done, Noah held her for several minutes until she slept, then placed her in her cradle.

"Are you sure about this?" he asked, turning back.

"Why wouldn't I be?"

"We haven't… I mean, you just had a baby a few weeks ago."

"Doc Martin said as long as it didn't hurt, it was okay."

"The doctor talked about this?"

"He is a doctor. We are married."

"Real slow then, and you'll tell me if it hurts."

"I will."

He eased out of his shirt and trousers, coming to lie beside her.

He was so warm and so strong and he felt so good against her. She'd always felt safe with him. Now he aroused her body, as well, but she wanted to feel more. She wanted to feel loved and desired.

"You feel so much smaller," he said, wrapping her close and running his hands over her.

"I *am* smaller," she laughed. And then when he cupped her breast, she added, "Except there."

"Is this okay?"

"They're sensitive, but I like that. Kiss me."

He was gentle and she appreciated that. He was focused and his determination drove her senses wild. She tried to touch him, return the caresses, but he purposefully pressed her hands to her sides and took his sweet time arousing her, tasting her, and—if she recognized it correctly—enjoying her.

He brought her to release twice before easing

himself over her and joining their bodies. "Does it hurt?" he asked.

Only to know he didn't feel for her the way she wanted him to. "No."

He threaded the fingers of both hands through hers and leaned on his elbows to lessen the burden of his weight, though she wouldn't have minded all of it.

"Please," she whispered, and her plea was hoarse. "Let me touch you."

He released her hands and she threaded her fingers into his hair, framed his face, brought him down for a kiss and held him fast.

Losing his well-guarded composure, he throbbed into her and groaned. He held her fast, lowered his face into her neck and sighed, "Katy…."

He'd called her that only a few times…only when he'd unconsciously dropped the protective formality he kept wedged between them. "I like it when you call me that."

It took only a few minutes for Noah to react to what had happened. She'd done this out of her sense of obligation. She'd told him a dozen times how grateful she was to be here, how she wanted to earn her way. He could stand anything but her pity. He was ashamed that he was so greedy for her that he let this happen. He loved the way she made him feel and hated himself for feeling it at the same time.

He eased himself away from her.

"Stay," she said sleepily, and rolled to her side.

He sat on the bed's edge. "I can't."

"Or you won't."

"I've told you. I can't be who you want me to be."

She sat. "I don't understand that."

"I'm sorry you don't 'cause this is the way it is." He got up and pulled on his trousers.

"You're sorry we did this, too, aren't you?"

"It just makes things more difficult."

"What things, Noah?"

He didn't answer.

"I'm a simple woman," she said. "I have simple needs."

"No. No, you don't."

"Do I ask so much of you?"

"You hardly ask for anything. But the things you do ask, I can't provide." She wanted a husband like other women had. A man who'd take her to town and accompany her to social events.

It wasn't much to ask. But it was everything. Too much.

"I see," she said, her voice sad. "I will try to be less demanding."

"You're not demanding. And you can't pretend to want less."

"I would be satisfied if I knew you were at peace with us."

"I don't know what peace is."

"I'm sorry for that."

He picked up his shirt. "Don't ever be sorry for me. I don't need your pity."

"I don't pity you."

He didn't believe her. Without responding to that, he walked to the door. "Good night, Katherine."

Chapter Thirteen

Rose woke her early. Kate climbed from the rumpled bed and donned her housecoat to run out to the privy and back. She gathered the baby and nestled back into bed while she nursed.

Last night Noah had declared that he would not provide what she wanted. Meaning the family she desired. Meaning the love she craved. Meaning this was all there'd ever be, and he didn't especially want the physical aspect of it, either. It made things more difficult.

How could she live here and accept his generosity without giving anything in return? Without feeling that she contributed, that she belonged, that she was desired and wanted?

What had she imagined all those months ago

in April when she'd climbed on his horse and ridden off? She'd taken a chance. Hoped for a better life. And she had one here.

She had to accept that things were as good as they would ever be—and they were awfully good—and that a romantic relationship was not in her future here. She would not make things more difficult for Noah by expecting or hoping for more. Seeing him with Rose, knowing Rose was provided for and loved, was all she needed.

Kate vowed to accept things as they were.

Annie asked her a week or so later if anything was troubling her. They were sharing a cup of tea in Annie's store and Rose was sleeping in a tiny crib that usually held a display of stockings.

"Nothing. Why do you ask?"

"You seem quieter than usual. Not yourself."

"No, I'm fine."

Marjorie asked her, too, from time to time, and even Noah stopped her on her way up to bed one evening.

"Katherine, is there something wrong?"

"Nothing—why do you ask?"

"You haven't joined me on the porch in the evening."

"I thought you would like the time alone with Rose."

"I do, but…well, I just wondered. You're awfully quiet."

"Perhaps I'm just a little tired."

"Rest then."

"I will. Good night."

She didn't have much energy for a few days. Taking care of Rose and doing a few simple tasks seemed to wear her out. She lay on her bed one evening, and there was a tap at the door.

"Yes?"

"May I come in?"

"Yes. What is it?"

"Are you sick, Katherine?" Noah came to the side of her bed and looked down at her. He bent to touch her face. "You have a fever."

"Do I? I can't tell. It's always warm up here of an afternoon."

"It's cooled off now that it's evening. I'll send for Doc Martin."

"I'm sure I'll feel better tomorrow."

"He'll see you anyway. What if it's something Rose could catch?"

"Oh!" Her heart raced at the thought. "Do you think so?"

"I don't know. Rest and I'll send for him."

She slept fitfully and woke when the doctor entered the room. He examined her while Noah waited in the hallway, then Doc asked him in.

"She doesn't have a rash of any kind. I don't think she's contagious, but we can't be sure. Katherine, it's probably best if you let someone else care for the baby until the fever is gone."

Kate's chest ached and ready tears sprang to her eyes. "Of course. I don't want her sick."

"I'm leaving medicine for you. Noah will make sure you take it. Just get plenty of rest and drink water."

Once the doctor was gone, Noah sat on the chair nearby and glanced at the baby in her cradle. "What shall we do? I can help, but I don't know much about babies."

"You have a ranch to run. How about asking Annie?"

"She would care for Rose I'm sure, but she has her own family. She'd have to take her home with her."

The thought was too disturbing. "No, that won't do. Marjorie then?"

"I'll send a hand to their place right now."

Three-fourths of an hour later, Harper Kimble returned from a ride to the Bensons with news that Marjorie was feeling poorly herself.

Kate ran a hand over her face when Noah gave her the report. Her head had begun to hurt so badly she could hardly think straight. "I guess we don't have any choice then."

"Estelle?" he asked.

She nodded.

He strode from the room.

During the night, she remembered Noah placing cool cloths on her head. Twice he brought Rose to her to nurse and then took her away.

She woke late the next morning and stared at the place where the cradle should have been.

Estelle entered the room with a bowl of water and toweling.

"Is Rose all right?"

"She's just fine. She's had her bath and is napping. Let's get you washed and change your nightdress and bedding. You've soaked everything clean through."

"Thank you, Estelle."

"I appreciate your wisdom in sending for me. Rose is my granddaughter, after all."

Kate's fever burned for two more days. Time became distorted and she could barely raise her head off the pillows. Disjointed dreams meshed with reality to make her even more confused.

Sometimes she heard Estelle and Noah talking about her, plotting and planning. Once Rose's pitiful cry was so near and so vivid, she fell trying to get to her. Levi was there and he was within reach of the baby, but he wouldn't reach for her. Her mother's voice kept taunting her that she was getting what she deserved, getting what she deserved....

"She's here and we have Levi's child," Estelle said. "The baby is the reason I told you to marry her. We won't lose Rose now."

She couldn't tell what Noah replied, but he didn't deny Estelle's claim.

Kate opened her eyes and the light hurt her head. She squinted and oriented herself in her room. Her breasts were painfully full.

In the overstuffed chair, Noah slept with his neck at an awkward angle. He raised his head when she sat up.

"Where's Rose?"

"Downstairs with Estelle."

"She's okay?"

"She's fine."

"No fever?"

"None."

"She hasn't nursed."

"You slept so hard, we gave her goat's milk through the night."

Kate couldn't bear to think Rose didn't need her. "May I see her now?"

Noah got up and left, returning a few minutes later with Rose bundled tightly in the flannel blankets Estelle set store by.

Kate freed the baby's legs and held her close.

Rose fretted and rooted for Kate's breast.

Kate opened her gown and grimaced in pain at the first hearty tugs, but then relaxed and drank in her baby with her eyes. She cradled her head and blinked back tears.

"How long have I been like this?"

"Most of a week now. Last night you called Levi's name."

Kate looked up and frowned. She vaguely remembered the nightmares. What had been real and what hadn't? "I heard you talking."

"What?"

"Did Estelle tell you to marry me?"

A guilty expression crossed his face. "She doesn't tell me what to do."

"But she put the idea in your head?"

"She mentioned it."

"Just like she mentioned to me that we weren't legally wed until the marriage was consummated."

A scowl revealed his displeasure, but he said nothing.

"Well, it worked," she said. "The two of you have Rose now. She's what you wanted. You don't want me. I was always the unpleasant means to get to Levi's child. Too bad I survived. I'm still in the way."

"That's not true. The fever is making you talk crazy."

"I want to be alone with my baby."

Noah turned and strode out of the room, closing the door behind him.

Angry voices rose from below, though Kate couldn't make out the words. She had never cried so much in her life. Her downcast state couldn't be good for her baby. She'd never felt so awful, either. Her head still pounded. Kate found her bottle of medicine and swallowed a spoonful.

Later, through a haze of fever, she saw Estelle come for Rose. Kate hadn't even heard her crying.

She woke again during the night. Her arms were empty. Her bed was empty and the cradle was still gone. They had what they wanted. Both of them—all they'd ever wanted was to make sure Levi's baby was here with them.

Neither of them wanted her. She'd just been part and parcel of the package. Until now.

She wasn't thinking clearly, that was a fact, but she knew enough to know when she was in the way.

They loved Rose. Everyone adored her. Rose would be taken care of and provided for. In a daze, Kate looked around her room. She'd brought nothing with her. None of this. In the whole house she'd provided a few napkins and eight china plates. In all the months she'd been here, she'd contributed nothing.

She'd heard stories of women who ran off and left their children, and she'd never understood. She'd always thought they didn't love their babies. She loved Rose with all her heart, but Rose wasn't old enough to love her back, wasn't old enough to miss her. Rose would be loved and cared for.

Kate felt her way down the stairs and out the front door. She'd never been in the barn and didn't have the vaguest idea how to saddle a horse, so she stumbled away from the house on foot. The cool night air felt good on her heated skin. The breeze ruffled her hair.

She didn't think about where she was going. She was leaving and that was her driving motivation. Getting away.

Noah woke at dawn and looked at his pocket watch. He'd fallen asleep across the foot of his bed and couldn't remember giving Katherine her medicine.

He washed, changed clothing and made his way to her room. The door was open and he rapped with one knuckle before entering. "Katherine?"

She wasn't in the bed or anywhere else in the room. Had she felt well enough to get up and dress?

He headed down the stairs, lightheartedly anticipating seeing her in the kitchen. Estelle was alone in the kitchen, bathing Rose in an enamel basin.

"Where's Katherine?"

"I have no idea."

"What do you mean? Did you see her this morning?"

"I haven't seen her since last night."

"You didn't check on her when you got up?" Alarmed now, Noah checked the perimeter of the house, the privy, ran back up and assessed her room more critically. Nothing was missing that he could tell, not even her shoes, which sat just under the edge of the bureau.

Her comb and brush lay on top, a ribbon strewn across the mirror.

Something was wrong. Panic welled in his chest.

He ran down the stairs and out to the bunkhouse where Newt and Harper were just heading out.

"What's wrong, boss?" Newt asked.

"Katherine's gone. I've looked everywhere."

"What about the baby?"

"Estelle has the baby. We have to find Katy."

A hundred images thrummed through his head. He should have stayed right there with her as he'd done the previous nights, but he'd been angry at her accusation that he had only wanted Levi's child and not her. Tired and frustrated, as well, but none of those were reason enough to leave her unprotected.

"Harper, you check the barn and stables and all the outbuildings. Newt, take a couple men and start searching out here. I'll take a couple with me to check the roads."

The hands shot to follow orders. Noah called to Jump and Lucky to saddle horses.

Not knowing where she was or what had happened to her drove knives into his heart. He hadn't heard anything during the night, no sounds of a struggle. He shouldn't have left her alone—he'd known she was ill and not herself. He shouldn't have gotten so defensive when she'd said he only wanted Levi's child.

He'd thought it at one time himself, but had it ever been true? Even from the very start? Something had made him gather her up and pack her off the day he'd met her. He'd convinced himself his concern was for the child, but everything had changed in the time she'd been at the Rockin' C. He couldn't imagine life without her.

She frightened him, yes, because he frightened himself. He'd lived a carefully constructed, protected life before she'd come, and the man who'd always shut out everything and everyone against the certainty of rejection had been slipping away. He'd been unprepared for the changes in himself.

As his life spun more and more out of control, he'd had to take second looks at the person he'd become and he didn't like him much.

He looked for signs of travel along the road, not seeing anything out of the ordinary. Jump and Lucky were spread out in the pastures on either side of him, riding slowly.

Ahead in the road, something white fluttered in the wind, catching his attention. Noah urged his horse into a gallop. Getting closer, he made out the form lying still, the hem of her white nightdress billowing around her legs.

"Katy!" He vaulted from his horse and ran to where she lay. "I found her!" Her face, arms, legs and feet were bare to the sun. Blood was caked on the bottom of her feet and her cotton nightdress was dirty.

Noah turned her face toward him and her eyelids fluttered, but she didn't open her eyes.

A pulse beat at the base of her throat, and he was never so glad to see something. He picked her up and pressed his cheek to her dirty tear-stained one.

Jump and Lucky reined in on either side of him. "She alive, boss?" Lucky asked.

He nodded. "I'm taking her to Doc's. Head on back."

Jump got down and held Katherine while Noah mounted his horse, then he handed the limp woman up to him.

Her unresponsiveness frightened Noah. Holding her close, he rode toward town.

It was an unusual sight, no doubt, a big bearded man on a horse carrying an unconscious woman in a nightgown. He was accustomed to stares, but they didn't even register now. All that mattered was getting his wife to the doctor's.

He took the straightest route down Main Street and turned, locating the doctor's little house set back on a street lined with trees. He swung one leg over the horse's back and slid to the ground.

A woman answered the bell. "Oh, goodness, bring her right in."

Doc Martin appeared and ushered Noah into a tiny bedroom. "Lay her down. What happened?"

"Don't know. She wasn't in her room and I found her along the road."

Doc looked her over. "Her feet are cut and bruised. She has a couple of scrapes on her knees. Her head's fine. The fever is back."

"She seemed better yesterday. I left her alone last night. I shouldn't have."

"This isn't your fault, Noah. A fever causes delirium sometimes. You thought she was better."

He nodded. "She'll be all right?"

"Can't rightly say till she wakes up, but no reason to think she won't."

"Can I stay with her?"

Doc turned a kind gaze his way. "Man has a right to stay with his wife. I'll get these cuts cleaned."

Once Katherine's cuts were washed and bandaged, Noah propped her shoulders while Doc's wife spooned water between her lips. The silver-haired woman washed Kate's face and hands and arms and tucked a sheet around her.

"She just needs to rest and fight the fever

now," she told him. She picked up a basin and towels and left, closing the door behind her.

Noah moved to sit on the edge of the bed and cradle Katherine's hand. He held her fingers to his lips. "I don't know if you can hear me, Katy," he said softly. "But I'm here. Get better, please?"

He stroked the back of her hand, her fingers where she wore a solitary gold band. *His wife,* he thought, and his throat closed. He wished now that he'd asked her about it when he'd noticed she had removed Levi's ring. He hadn't let himself think about it after noticing. He'd been afraid of reading too much into it. But the fact that she now wore only his ring had given him secret pleasure.

Had she considered those two rings as often as he had? Could she have known how much it would mean to him, the meaning he would derive from her removing it? If she had, she'd once again been the one to make an effort.

Kate was a doer. She went after what she wanted.

Noah was an avoider. But he needed to do something now. Something to help her. Feeling helpless, he laid his forehead on her hand for a moment and an idea came to him.

"I'll be right back. I promise."

He settled his hat on his head, strode out of the house and mounted his horse. A few people noticed him as he rode toward the church, but he kept going. When he reached the house with roses climbing the arbor, he dismounted, walked the brick path to the door and knocked.

Mrs. Davidson appeared and smiled. "Mr. Cutter, what a surprise this is. Won't you come in?"

Hesitantly he crossed the threshold into her front hallway. Manners dictated he remove his hat, so he did so.

She looked at him with a measure of surprise.

"I need to speak with the reverend, ma'am."

"Certainly. He's in the kitchen, reading the newspaper. Go right in."

Noah hadn't been in another person's house for years, and he couldn't help noticing the women's touches missing from his. He found Reverend Davidson at the kitchen table with a cup of coffee.

"Noah!" he said, looking up in surprise. "What a pleasant surprise."

"I've come to ask a favor."

"What is it?"

"It's for my wife. Katherine. She's sick. Fever. I was wondering if…well…"

"What're you wanting to ask me?"

"It'd mean a lot to her if you came and said a prayer."

"It would be my privilege. I'll ride out this afternoon."

"No, she's at Doc Martin's and I think you should come now."

"Very well." He removed his eyeglasses and folded the ear pieces. "Let's go."

Noah believed she'd heard the prayer Reverend Davidson had spoken over her. She'd seemed more peaceful afterward.

That evening as he sat beside her, he sensed a change. He took her hand and, finding it cooler, touched her cheek.

He moved to the door and called softly for the doctor.

Doc entered the room.

"She's cool."

Doc touched her head. "So she is. Now we wait for her to wake up."

Mrs. Martin brought Noah a bedroll and he stretched out on the floor. He'd have slept in the chair, but this would save his back and neck a night of torture.

"Get a good night's sleep, Katy," he said. "It's real odd not hearing you talk. I like it, you know, everything you have to say. You always look on the good side of things. You make me stop and see things in a way I never have before. You show me color where I never saw it. That's a rare quality."

He thought of the way she talked about the sky and the stars. "When you're better, we'll go out and look at the stars at night. You like that."

He got up and knelt beside her bed, reached up and stroked her soft cheek with the back of a knuckle. "I guess I'd do just about anything to have you well. To see your smile and hear you chatter on like a magpie."

His life had been better and fuller since Katherine had come into it. Her silence frightened him. He thought of the few things she'd ever asked of him, and instead of hating himself for being unable to change, he made up his mind he was stronger than that. But was he a strong enough man to be the man she wanted him to be?

He'd been lying to himself all along in believing that he wanted Levi's child. He'd come to love Rose, of course, but from the very first it had been Katy he wanted.

"Wake up, Katy," he said against her cheek. "So I can show you I can change."

When the pain finally subsided from Kate's head, her feet and her breasts throbbed. Why in the world did her feet hurt so? She cracked open her eyes. The rose wallpaper and chintz print curtain were unfamiliar. The room was tiny and there was a crack across the plaster ceiling.

This was not her room.

She opened her eyes wide. Fear stole her breath. "Where am I?"

"Doc's place." Noah's voice. "You've been sick."

She looked into his kind eyes and found reassurance. She glanced around again. Moved her sore feet. Touched her engorged breasts.

"Rose is here, too. She's been waiting for

you to wake up." He came to sit on the edge of the bed.

She remembered hearing his voice, his words of encouragement and promise through the haze of her dreamworld. He'd been asking her to wake up. "You were talking to me."

He nodded. "Yes."

"How did I get here?"

He told her what had happened, but she had only a vague recollection, as though it had all been a disjointed dream.

She thought back to the day the doctor had come to the house. "How is Marjorie? She wasn't feeling well, either."

"Tipper stopped by yesterday. Said she was afraid she had a similar ailment, but turns out she's going to have a baby."

"Oh, my." Tipper and Marjorie had been married nearly ten years without a child. "Well... well, that's wonderful. I think it's wonderful, anyway. Are they happy?"

"Wore a sappy grin, he did."

She inched up a little on the pillows. "You said Rose is here?" Her baby had been without her all this time. The thought broke her heart. "Who's taking care of her? How long has it been?"

"You've been sick a few days. I had Estelle bring her here. I'll go get her."

At the mention of Estelle, Kate's worries intensified. She hated that the woman had been their only choice to care for the baby during her illness. She didn't want to see her.

Kate didn't have to worry about it right then. Noah carried Rose in to Kate on his own and placed the baby in her arms.

It seemed her child had grown and gained weight while Kate had been unaware. She should be grateful that Estelle had cared for her so well, but instead she felt resentful that they could get by without her. Rose was sleeping and Kate snuggled her close, love and possessiveness rising up in her. At the sweet smell of her baby, her breasts ached.

Noah pulled a straight chair close to the bed and seated himself beside her. "Things are going to be different from now on," he said.

"What do you mean?"

"I'm sending Estelle home again today. I've thanked her for her help, because she did help. But we're not falling back into letting her interfere."

A wave of relief washed over Kate at his words. "Thank you for that."

"Other things will change, too."

"What things?"

"I was wrong…when I said you'd have to learn to accept me the way I was."

"I was wrong, too—"

"No. You were accepting of me all along. I just didn't let you."

She tried to understand.

"We both want the same thing," he said.

"Rose?"

He tilted his head to acknowledge that was so, but added, "A family."

She knew how much it meant for him to have Levi's daughter. To know that she would inherit a share of the ranch. Kate had no doubt indicated that wish in a dozen ways if not in so many words. But pushing her desires on him wasn't fair. His sense of duty and responsibility would require him to do anything she asked. And that wasn't fair.

"You've given me so much," she told him.

"There was a time when I didn't have hope for a good life for Rose."

Kate had always felt that her mother resented her, and her mother had never made it a secret that she'd had no use for Kate's father. She'd drilled it into Kate that her life was hard because of the man and because she'd had to take care of a child alone.

Seeing herself thrust into the very same situation had terrified her. She hadn't want to become a bitter resentful mother. She had grown up without love and acceptance and she didn't want to impose that type of survival on another child.

"What you've provided for us is enough," she told Noah. "I'm not ungrateful."

Her mother hadn't really loved her, not enough to lay down blame and resentment. Kate had thought for a few brief weeks that Levi had loved her, but his interest had been all about the sex.

Kate faced the cold, hard fact that she couldn't make Noah or Estelle love her, either. She had to accept that no one was going to love her.

She could live with that. As along as Rose was loved and accepted.

"It's going to work out, Noah."

She would make it so.

Chapter Fourteen

Estelle did come for a short visit. Kate thanked her for taking care of Rose.

"I was glad to do it, dear. You know you can call on me anytime."

"That's comforting to know."

Noah told Estelle when it was time to go, and she gathered her skirts and whisked past him.

Annie visited her, too, bringing her a bottle of rose water. Kate unscrewed the cap. The scent immediately reminded her of Noah and his roses. The delicate fragrance had become a familiar comfort and it reminded her of her new home.

"I want to go home," she told Annie, and her friend went to get Noah.

"He's gone to get his buggy." Annie gathered Kate's belongings. "It's so good to know you're feeling better. We were all worried. I was concerned you'd be asleep for so long your milk would dry up."

"Before I got so bad, Estelle was bringing Rose to me."

"Thank God."

Kate realized then that if Estelle had had any mean intentions toward her, she could have kept the baby away entirely, but she hadn't. On the other hand, she knew breast milk was best for Rose.

Once Kate was dressed, they found the doctor and his wife in a parlor near the front door.

Annie insisted Kate sit on a chair while she held Rose.

"Your husband has been so attentive to your needs," Mrs. Martin told Kate. "Can't say I ever knew the man before this. Knew he lived out there and heard the tales, of course—most of them farfetched, I can see now. He's a good man."

It came to Kate then that Noah had been interacting with these people for the past couple of days. Another thought struck her, and she turned to Annie. "You said he went to get the buggy?"

"Yes."

"At Luke's livery."

Annie nodded.

"Why, it's right in town. He's been in town these past days."

Annie nodded, as did Mrs. Martin.

Noah avoided setting foot in town at all costs. The fact that he was here now amazed her.

"He went for the preacher, too," Doc told her.

"He did?"

He nodded. "Brought Reverend Davidson right here to your bedside to pray over you."

She was grateful, but she couldn't get too excited over something that didn't need more written into it than was there. "He lost his mother when he was very young," Kate told them. "I'm sure he was afraid that the same thing might happen to Rose."

"Well, thanks to God and medicine, you're just fine." Annie leaned over to give her a hug.

Mrs. Martin moved aside her curtains to announce, "He's here."

Kate thanked her before Doc and Annie

walked her outside. Noah jumped down and helped Kate into the buggy. Annie kissed Rose's forehead and handed her over. "I'll come see you," she called.

Noah seated himself beside Kate and lifted the reins over the horses's backs.

Kate was relieved to get back to the house. Marjorie fussed over her, but within a few days she was up and around, feeling better physically now that September was drawing to a close than she had in months.

She had Rose to take care of, and she loved her duties feeding, bathing, changing. But babies sleep a lot and during those times, she was back to searching for ways to occupy her mind and hands.

Fall transformed the mountains into glorious displays of color. Kate admired the aspens from the porch and her bedroom window at least a dozen times a day. Noah had cut the last of the roses and she'd placed them in a jar of water on the kitchen table. There were any number of small pleasures to enjoy in a day. Kate never forgot to be thankful for her new home.

She had determined—and she was a very determined woman—that it was enough.

* * *

When Kate had been so ill, Noah had realized that his solitary day-to-day existence was not enough. He'd settled for less, because he'd never dreamed he could have more, but Kate had given him the gift of hope.

He'd told her he wanted a family, and she'd agreed her desire was the same. Still, acceptance was only one part of their relationship and he cautioned himself not to dream that love would ever be in the equation.

With the oppressive summer heat gone, days were comfortable and nights downright cool. Their evenings together were now spent in the parlor with a fire warming the room. Kate sewed while Noah held and rocked Rose. He came in earlier than he had when he'd been trying to avoid her. He'd made up his mind to be the man she needed and wanted, and to do that he had to change.

Nearly losing Kate had shown him what he had and what he'd been resisting all along, and he was determined to show her he could be the man she wanted. This part, the family part, was easy. He loved Rose and her sweet baby smell. Whenever she saw him, her eyes lit up and a toothless smile broke across her chubby face. She was as accepting as he'd once only hoped.

"We should take advantage of the warm days left. Shall we have a picnic tomorrow?" he asked Kate.

She glanced up, her expression interested. "Do you have time?"

He nodded. "It will be Rose's first picnic."

"She has the pram you ordered for her. We'll take it along for shade."

Kate put away her sewing and went into the kitchen, returning with a pail of water. "I'll pour these in our basins, if you will carry Rose."

"My pleasure."

After placing the baby in her cradle, he went to his room and washed. Since Kate's illness, he hadn't gone to her room. Changing was going to take every ounce of courage he possessed. But he couldn't continue his life the way it had been, not if he wanted more. Not if he wanted Katy. And he did.

Dressed only in his denims, he approached her door and knocked.

A minute later the light visible through the crack along the floor disappeared and she called for him to enter. Maybe it wasn't entirely for his benefit that she darkened the room. Maybe she didn't want to see. His stomach felt uneasy. Maybe it was easier to endure his attentions in the dark.

She said what she thought, however. Unless it was unkind and she thought the truth would hurt his feelings. If he tested her distaste, what would he learn?

Choosing to make a change, no matter how difficult, he found his way to the bureau and located the tin of matches by feel. He struck one and relit the lantern. The wick was set so that a low glow illuminated the room, creating long shadows.

He turned to find her watching him curiously from where she perched on the edge of the bed. He walked toward her and her gaze lowered from his face to his chest.

It wasn't daylight, he told himself when he wanted to turn away. She could barely see the scars she'd already felt and knew existed.

"Tell me what you're thinking," he said.

She shook her head.

"Why not?"

"You'll be angry with me."

"You're thinking I'm not much compared to Levi."

Her eyes widened and she stared up at him. "No. No, I'd never think that."

"What then? What would make me angry?"

"I was thinking about the way you've hidden all these years, and it makes me sad."

"You couldn't say that?"

"You called it pity last time I mentioned what I was thinking, though that's not what I'm doing—pitying you. A person can't help feeling…*sorrow*…or regret when they imagine another person's feelings."

"So you're feeling sorry for me?"

She looked away.

"Say it. You feel sorry for me."

"No, Noah." She met his eyes. "You do enough of that yourself."

If she'd struck him, he couldn't have been more surprised. He stood in front of her, absorbing her words and their meaning. Feeling sorry for himself? Is that what he'd been doing? The accusation made him angry, but denial wasn't ready on his lips.

The more he thought about it, the more he understood what she'd just revealed. He'd been counting on her to say what she thought, but he hadn't been expecting that.

"Maybe there's some truth in that," he admitted finally.

"I didn't make you mad?"

"Always tell me the truth, no matter what."

"All right."

He eased beside her onto the bed and she turned to face him. He loved the way she looked at him with trust in her eyes. He stroked her cheek, loving the satiny feel. Her braid lay across her breast, calling his attention to her thin nightdress.

Noah leaned forward to kiss her and she raised a palm to his shoulder. Within moments the sweet blaze of passion drove him to deepen the kiss.

He filled his hand with the weight of her breast and she met him kiss for kiss, touch for touch.

"Is it easier for you in the dark?" he asked.

"You're the one who preferred darkness."

Against her cheek he asked, "Do you imagine I'm Levi?"

Her body stiffened and she inched back to

stare at him. "What a dreadful thing to say. Do you imagine I'm someone else?"

"Of course not. You're perfect. Beautiful. I can't imagine anything better."

She looked stunned at those words and blinked up at him.

"You have something to compare," he insisted. "I doubt I equal my brother."

"You think I'm beautiful?"

He skimmed her jaw with the backs of his fingers. "Sometimes just looking at you hurts."

"I never knew."

"That you're beautiful? How could you not know? Didn't Levi tell you?"

"Levi told me a lot of things that weren't true. That's what I have to compare you to, Noah. A whole pack of lies and empty promises."

"I'm sorry for what he did to you."

"You had nothing to do with it. Even so, you took responsibility for us, Rose and I. That's more than Levi did."

"The fact that I'm taking care of you dulls the unpleasantness of my appearance, I'm sure."

She pulled away completely and sat up. "So I'd be here in bed with any man who would've been willing to 'take care of me'?"

"I didn't say that."

"You suggested that I pretend you're someone else and overlook your scars so that you will take care of me."

"You have it all twisted now."

"No, *you* have it all twisted."

Noah caught himself before he replied. He'd been determined to change, but here he was asking her to compare him to his brother, feeling less. Feeling inadequate. As always. He should be proving to her he was the best man despite his looks. "Sorry, Katy. In my head I'm so sure of what you're thinking that I don't let you tell me."

She scooted back on the bed, wrapped her arms around her raised knees and looked at him. His first instinct was to hide, to turn away, to douse the lamp, but he sat under her perusal.

"You told me once not to tell you what you're thinking, do you remember?"

He nodded.

"But you assume what I'm thinking, don't you?"

Again he nodded.

"What am I thinking right now?"

He glanced at her toes peeking from beneath

her nightdress, then back to her face. Her gaze traveled from his eyes to his chest and shoulders. "I only know what I think when I see myself," he said finally. "And I'm disgusted."

"I'm thinking I wish I could see you better. So I'd know what it is you think it so terrible that I'll turn away."

"I guess that's the chance I wasn't willing to take." He got up, found the match tin and carried it to the lamp on the wall inside the door. "Will the light wake Rose?"

Katherine glanced to where the baby lay sleeping in her cradle. "I don't think so."

Having an idea, Noah moved the dressing screen so that it shaded the baby and struck a match. The smell of sulfur permeated the room and once he lit the lamp, the tin reflector spread the glow.

He felt her gaze on him as he returned the match tin to the bureau and returned to the bed. With uncertainty, he looked for her reaction. It took all his determination not to flinch and turn away.

She wore a half smile. "I'm thinking you look strong. I like the width of your shoulders. And the muscles across your chest."

He came forward slowly and sat beside her.

"The focus isn't all on those scars, Noah. Once a person has seen them and experienced the initial questions, they just don't matter much anymore. Every time I look at you I won't be thinking the same things I thought the first time."

He'd never thought that far ahead because he'd never wanted anyone to see him in the first place. But she was right. She had to be.

Now that he thought back, she had never treated him as though she couldn't bear the sight of him. She'd been accepting while he couldn't accept himself. She'd been okay with him the way he was until he'd made her not okay.

She moved behind him and rose to her knees. She worked magic along his neck and shoulders with her hands. "When I look at you, I see strength and honor and courage. I don't see scars."

"How can that be?"

"Maybe because I'm not looking for them. Or because I'm looking past them. I can't explain it."

She delved her fingers into his hair and

stroked his scalp. He tipped his head to look up at her and she leaned forward to frame his face. The kiss they shared was awkward until Noah shifted, stretching out and pulling her down on top of him.

Nothing was awkward after he framed her face with his hands and kissed her the way she liked. As their passion grew, he slid both hands under her nightdress so he could enjoy her satiny hips and stroke her back.

Katherine sat up and tugged the garment over her head, tossing it to the floor.

Noah drank in the sight of her in the lantern light. Her shoulders were sleek and pale, her breasts full and lush. "Katy," he breathed.

She curled her fingers into the hair on his belly and tilted her head as though to ask a question.

"You're as beautiful as I pictured in my head. Better."

Even her smile was seductive. "I like it when you call me 'Katy.'"

Once he'd thought he would call her Katy if he were a different man. Now he realized he'd been thinking of her that way for some time.

The significance was not lost on him. "Katy," he said again.

She leaned forward to kiss him and he captured her breasts.

"Katy," he breathed between kisses.

"You do want me like this, Noah?"

Her question didn't register in his head for a moment. "Like what?"

"In this way. For lovemaking."

"How could you think anything else?"

"I don't know. At first you were reluctant. I felt like…like you were doing it because it was just another of your duties, not because you wanted to."

"I want to."

"I want you to need me."

He hadn't expected to need anyone this way. She was sustenance and life to his once-deprived soul. "I do. I need you so much it hurts."

He took his fill of looking at her. He touched and kissed each delectable sight, tasting her skin, loving her sighs and whispers. There were few activities during which Katy didn't talk. He'd discovered them all: while she slept; early in the morning; and those tense drawn-out moments before he brought her release.

Afterward, Noah lay on his back, the sheet draped over his groin, and allowed Kate to see the scars on his legs.

"Turn over," she said, and he obeyed.

She straddled him and massaged his back and shoulders, then moved aside and pulled the sheet down to look at the rest of him.

"You've seen it all," he said.

"Almost."

He frowned. "What else?"

She urged him onto his back and threaded his hair away from his face, then studied him.

It was all he could do not to turn aside, but he fought back his instincts and let her look. And waited for a reaction.

"Thank you," she said finally.

"For what?"

"For trusting me this much."

Trusting her. Of course. He'd always expected a superficial reaction, and that's what he'd always gotten. Katy knew him better than anyone except Levi ever had. He'd had to be willing to trust her to see more than the surface, and he hadn't.

She got up and found her nightdress on the floor and pulled it over her head. He'd enjoyed the view until she turned down the wicks so that the lights were extinguished, then moved the dressing screen away from the cradle. "She's still sound asleep."

Climbing back into the bed, she snuggled against him and he turned to accommodate her, tucking her bottom against his abdomen. Within moments he slept.

Kate woke to feed Rose during the night, and Noah still slept soundly, so she didn't disturb him. He woke while it was still dark and sat.

She rolled onto her back to peer at him.

"Morning," he said and moved to the edge of the bed.

"What time is it? I'll go get water."

"No. I'll go. You stay here. You need your rest."

"What about you?"

"I didn't just give birth to a baby and then have a raging fever for days." He turned to look at her. "Rest."

"All right."

She dozed until he brought her water. Then he carried the rest of the pail to his room.

Rose woke, so Kate fed her and then washed and dressed both of them for the day.

There was a bowl of oatmeal on the table and a kettle of hot water on the stove when she got downstairs. She brewed tea and ate part of the cereal. Sitting at the table in the deserted kitchen, the rest of the day loomed ahead of her. She decided to go into town to visit Annie.

That evening Noah was attentive to both her and Rose, and they quite naturally added another change. After their time together downstairs, Noah came to her room with her. Little by little, he moved his belongings until they were sharing a room.

Kate lived for the evenings and the nights and enjoyed her baby during the days. But she became more and more restless and less and less content with the way her marriage had evolved. She was not ungrateful. Nor did she expect more than Noah was willing to give.

All along she'd thought that if he simply needed her, it would make everything better. He had admitted he needed her. She was an eager and accommodating partner and enjoyed Noah's lovemaking. Thinking of what they shared as a trade for her keep cheapened it, but without more, what was sex really?

Noah seemed to sense her unrest and sometimes he mentioned that she was awfully quiet. He went out of his way to show her he had changed, and he had. But there was a strain, an underlying tension that remained.

The most shocking event thus far happened the following Sunday morning. Noah showed up in the kitchen dressed in the dark trousers and white shirt he'd worn to Levi's funeral.

Kate turned to stare. "Noah! What's this?"

"I'm dressed."

"I see that. For what?"

"For church. You asked me to go. I've decided I will."

She pressed a hand to her breast. "You look positively handsome in that shirt and tie. Why, you'll have all the women looking at you instead of at Reverend Davidson. I can hardly keep *my* eyes off."

His tanned cheeks deepened in color.

"Take Rose, will you please? I have to gather my hat and gloves."

Noah accepted the infant quite naturally, smiled down and touched her nose with a long finger. Rose gurgled her happiness to see him. The sight of him holding her baby touched a chord in Kate as it always did.

Noah was quiet on the ride to church, but Noah was always quiet. She knew how much courage it would take for him to remove his hat in church and let people look at him. As he drove, she grasped his forearm and tried to convey her pride. When he glanced at her she could offer only a smile.

Noah's arrival at church caused an initial stir as heads turned and the congregation wore various expressions of surprise. As all the men did, he removed his hat to hang it on a peg on the back wall. A few people stared outright just as Noah had told her they always had. The two of them walked down the aisle and Kate stared right back until the offending churchgoers caught themselves and looked away.

Several members shook Noah's hand and spoke to him: Luke and Annie, of course, the Sweetwaters and the Renlows, but also a few of the nearby ranchers.

When they reached the pew where Kate always sat with Estelle, the woman hadn't arrived yet. Kate and Noah settled in with Rose on Noah's lap, and Mrs. Davidson paused to say hello.

The crowd was buzzing with the usual early morning chatter when Estelle stopped at the end of the pew. She stared. Her mouth hung open until she snapped it shut.

"Good morning, Estelle," Kate addressed her.

The woman glanced around and, obviously not wanting to be a spectacle herself, stiffly inched her way in beside Kate and sat facing forward. "What is he doing here?" she whispered.

"Attending service, same as everyone else."

"What is he doing in my pew?"

"You told me once that this is the Cutter pew. Noah is a Cutter. By birth." After adding that last comment, she wanted to bite her tongue. But Estelle had her nerve and Kate would not let Noah be humiliated for doing something to please her.

The anger emanating from Estelle was almost palpable. All through the service, she stared straight ahead except when she asked Kate if she could hold Rose.

The service ended and Estelle handed the

baby back to Kate, popped up and hurried to the rear of the building.

Once the reverend had greeted Noah and Kate, they stepped out into the sunshine. Noah tucked on his hat, as did every other man. Gil Chapman, Luke's uncle and a local rancher, addressed him, and the two engaged in a conversation.

Charmaine and Annie joined Kate and admired Rose's bonnet.

"What a pleasure to see your husband here this morning." Annie gave Kate a warm hug.

"He surprised me this morning."

"I think this marriage is turning out to be more than you expected," her friend whispered.

"Maybe on my side," Kate admitted.

Annie gave her a sly smile. "I see the way he looks at you."

With a gloved hand, Kate waved away her teasing. She wasn't going to heap more expectations upon the man who married her out of duty. From the corner of her eye, she noticed someone move up beside her.

"Why did *he* come today?" Estelle asked.

Kate glanced to see the woman in her black dress, her face pinched and unforgiving.

Charmaine and Annie gave Kate and Estelle sidelong looks.

"Why does anyone attend church?" Kate replied kindly. "It's the Sabbath and a day of worship."

"People are staring." Estelle leaned closer. "He's repulsive. He doesn't belong in polite society."

Polite? Defensive anger welled in Kate. "I'm trying to remember that I just sang hymns and prayed, what a help you were when I was sick and that it's not fitting a lady to wallop another in the churchyard."

Estelle's face blanched and she blinked in surprise.

Charmaine gently took Kate's arm, but she ignored the censure. "I can't please you, Estelle, because I'm never going to be good enough, so I have nothing to lose no matter what I say now. You've treated Noah badly his entire life. He was young and had no mother of his own and you made him feel worthless. He needed love and compassion, but you didn't offer him any."

Estelle glanced at Annie, as though she'd find

support for her twisted thinking, but Annie stayed by Kate's side.

"He's not my son," Estelle sniffed.

Kate had let that comment pass for the last time. "No, thank goodness. I've never heard a good word come out of your mouth regarding Noah. He's the kindest, most honorable man I've ever met. *Your son,* on the other hand, was a liar and a cheat."

Estelle's chest puffed out and her face turned as red as a ripe tomato. "Why, you—you…" she stammered.

"I'm so blessed that Noah did the *honorable* thing and came for me. I'm glad he is the father Rose will know."

Kate knew she'd gone too far.

Charmaine put her arm around her shoulder, whether to shut her up or to protect her should Estelle suddenly fly into pieces, she didn't know.

Tears came to Estelle's eyes and she fumbled in the pocket of her skirt for a handkerchief, bringing it to her eyes and dabbing. "I expect poor manners from him, but you should be trying to elevate yourself. It's inexcusable to speak to me in such a disrespectful manner."

Kate wanted to say she had no respect for the woman, but she finally bit her tongue and resisted.

Estelle pinched her nose with the handkerchief and blotted it daintily. She looked at Rose before saying, "I'm going to excuse your behavior this time, because you were raised with little regard for proper conduct. We won't let this affect our visits."

"I don't have the right to tell you that your visits are unwelcome. The ranch and house are Noah's, not mine. And I don't know how Noah would feel about turning you away from your granddaughter. All I know is that I won't condone the way you speak to and about Noah. If you are going to be around my daughter, your treatment of him will have to change."

Annie moved away then, and Kate sensed a larger presence. She turned to see Noah standing beside her.

He met her eyes with an expression she imagined was admiration.

He looked at his stepmother. "Katy's word is

the authority regarding our home and visitors. She says you're welcome, so be it. She says no, I back her up."

Annie and Charmaine had slipped away from the confrontation once Noah arrived, and the three Cutters now stood to the side of the churchyard, Kate holding Rose.

Estelle looked long and hard at Rose, then forced her gaze up to Noah's. "Your father was broken-hearted, you know. He felt so guilty over what happened that day that he was never the same."

"He couldn't stand the sight of me any more than you could," Noah replied.

She shook her head. "No, he loved you deeply. He was riddled with remorse and couldn't bear to see what he considered to be his fault." She raised her chin a notch. "He kept all of your mother's belongings and wouldn't allow me to get rid of them. He used to visit her grave every day and talk to her as though she was still alive."

Noah wore a strange expression as though vaguely remembering.

"That's why I left," she said. "I wasn't going

to stay and compete with a dead woman and her son."

"My father loved you and Levi," Noah told her.

"Yes." She glanced away, blinking. "But he loved the two of you first. And better. I couldn't bear that."

"I understand being jealous. But I don't understand cruelty."

She gave her eyes a final dab and tucked the handkerchief into her pocket. "There are a lot of things you don't understand." She turned her gaze back to Kate. "Do I have your...permission to visit Rose?"

"Under the condition that you will always speak respectfully and kindly of Noah."

Her throat worked, and it was obvious it took all her fortitude to agree. "Very well."

She turned and made her way to where her driver waited by the black buggy. He assisted her up onto the seat and she rode away.

Noah took Kate's arm and led her to their own rig and horse, waiting in the shade.

They were well outside town when he at last spoke. "I thought he couldn't stand to look at me."

Kate reached over and took his hand. "It was his guilt eating him up."

"I guess I'd feel guilty, too. If it was my son."

"But you'd show him love and acceptance."

He nodded.

What a big day this had been. Kate was proud of Noah for what he'd done in going to church and showing the community that they were a family.

They'd come so far since she'd been here, since Reverend Davidson had pronounced them man and wife. Noah had even welcomed her as a lover.

One situation remained that kept her from feeling a hundred percent secure and important. He wanted her physically, yes, but Noah still didn't need her. Not really. He had all the things he'd always had, but now his life included a lover he hadn't chosen or asked for.

Kate determined to be happy with things the way they were. She could still find other ways to belong and make her place here. She had a lifetime.

In the days that followed, Noah digested the information regarding his father and his misinterpretation of his father's regret. So much of who he had turned out to be had hinged on other people's reactions to him and their avoidance.

Katy's acceptance had changed the way he felt about himself. He was thankful every day that she'd come into his life and shaken it up—for the better.

She'd been silent ever since the night before when she'd asked again if they could have a garden in the spring. The only time she'd spoken to him was that morning when she'd mentioned the possibility of her raising chickens and selling eggs.

"You don't have to pay your way here," he'd told her again. "We trade and have enough hands to make what we need."

At noon she placed bowls of stew on the table and sliced bread without speaking. Katy being silent was like the sun not coming up. He observed her with concern. "You feeling okay?"

"I'm fine."

"Stew's good."

"Fergie made it."

As he went about his chores that afternoon, he tried to figure out what was troubling her.

She'd grown less and less responsive ever since her illness, and he had chalked it up to getting back on her feet again, but she seemed in perfect physical health.

At supper he rearranged his dinnerware and sat beside her.

She smiled and touched his arm, but it was a sad smile.

Later, as they sat in the parlor, a fire crackling in the hearth, she sewed. "I've gotten quite skilled at these gowns for Rose," she said, holding one up for him to see.

"Looks nice."

"Annie doesn't have clothing for infants in her shop. Perhaps I could place a few for her to sell for me."

With Rose on his lap, he glanced up at her. "You don't—"

"Don't tell me," she said before he could finish. "I don't need to do that. We don't need the money. No one needs anything I have to offer."

She stuffed the fabric into the basket beside her chair and stood.

"Katy?"

She moved past him into the kitchen.

He got up and followed, the baby in the crook of his arm. "What's troubling you? I want you to tell me."

At the sink, she scrubbed at the two coffee mugs they'd used earlier.

"I'm not moving from this spot until you tell me what's wrong."

She turned and there were tears in her eyes. The sight did something to him that made his chest ache.

"You don't need me," she said.

"What? Of course I do."

"No." She slanted her head to emphasize. "You don't. Ever since I got here, I've tried to fit in, tried to find something that was just mine. A way to contribute."

"But you don't need to—"

"You see." She pointed at him with a wet finger. "That's exactly my point. That's what you say every time. I didn't need to learn to bake bread. I don't even have to cook or do dishes. I wouldn't have to do my own laundry or Rose's if I didn't insist, and I don't have to do anything else.

"I offered to take in laundry. I'd like to try a garden and grow our own vegetables. I just suggested making a few gowns to sell. I know you don't need any paltry offering I can make." Her voice trembled. "I know I don't have much to give."

Noah listened to her words and recognized his every denial. It was true he'd turned aside all those suggestions. He hadn't wanted her to do anything out of obligation.

She looked up at him, her hazel eyes dark and imploring. "I need to feel important."

Her plea came from her heart and it nearly broke his. That she felt this way was his wrongdoing. How had he made such a mess of things? "I tried to make your life easy. I was trying to make things up to you, I guess."

"That's not your place," she told him.

"I can see that now. Instead of making the way easy, I denied you things that would give you a sense of belonging."

She looked at him, her glistening eyes wide with relief.

"I'll probably make a lot more mistakes," he said. "Don't know much about women. About marriage. Just don't stop talking, Katy. I need you to talk."

A smile quivered on her lips.

He stepped to cup her cheek in his palm. "I need you to show me what's important. If it's important to you, it's important to me. You can do anything you want, anything you like. You can grow vegetables and sew little night-dresses. You can raise a flock of chickens and cook all the meals you like."

She brought her damp hand up to cover the back of his and looked into his eyes.

He leaned down to press a tender kiss against Kate's lips. He felt her tremble and pulled her close. Rose squirmed on his arm and fussed.

Kate pulled back to look at her baby. "She's probably ready to eat and go to bed."

"I'll be up in a few minutes," he told her.

Kate took Rose from him and carried her upstairs, where she lit lamps and changed the baby.

After Rose had nursed, Kate tucked her into her cradle and performed her own nightly ritual. It seemed to take Noah a long time to finish his chores. She lay down and closed her eyes, thinking over the things he'd said and the reassurance he'd given her.

She understood now that he'd wanted to pro-vide for her and to make her life easier, and she appreciated that. If he could only understand how much easier her life already was. But easy wasn't everything. Fulfilling and rewarding were just as important.

She'd drifted off to sleep when she heard footsteps and saw a tall, broad-shouldered man cross the room. She sat up in alarm.

He turned up the wick on the lamp and she clutched the bedclothes to herself, wondering who had so calmly walked in and made himself at home.

His clothing was familiar, as was the stride when he crossed to the bed where she sat.

"Katy?" Noah's voice.

He sat on the edge of the bed and she stared.

"Noah?" With a hand that shook, she reached up to touch his cheek.

His eyes closed and a muscle ticked in his jaw as though he steeled himself for a physical blow.

His cheeks were cleanly shaven, revealing a strong jaw and a full, sensitive mouth. The scars themselves were not pretty, and some might think they distracted from his handsome appearance, but she saw only the face of a kind, honorable, hurting man.

"So this is you," she said.

His eyes opened and he read her expression with uncertainty. "You tried to tell me a dozen times that you didn't feel needed. I was too dense to see that. Well, I do need you. I need you to love me," he said.

More than she'd ever hoped for. More than she'd dreamed and thought she'd never have. More than words could say or she could express was the part of himself that Noah offered now.

"I want to be the man you need."

Even though tears sprang to her eyes she got up on her knees and kissed him long and hard. Framing his face with both hands, she looked into the eyes of the man who'd given her everything.

"You are the man I need. I didn't ask you to do the things you've done, but you did them to prove your love for me. At first I didn't let myself hope that you had feelings for me, not more than pity or guilt or maybe even attraction, because I didn't want to love you and not have your love back.

"I thought you only wanted Levi's child, but what you did today...and what you've done now—" she stroked his cheek "—shows me you do care for me. I'm sorry I was such a dolt and…and I do love you, Noah. I've known it for a while. I think I knew it when I took off Levi's ring."

"I need you to know how important you are to me," he said.

She blinked through her tears and nodded. "Okay."

"I need you to keep making me see life in color and to show me all the good things I never took time to look at. I need you talk all the time and even tell me what I'm thinking."

She gave a little laugh and stroked his cheek.

"But mostly I need you to love me."

"I do. I love you." She kissed the scar at the corner of his mouth and the one near his eye. "You're thinking you love me, too." She inched away to look into his eyes expectantly.

"All along I thought Levi should have loved you," he said gruffly.

She smiled and waited.

"I loved you then, I guess," he said.

"And now?"

"I love you more now."

"And tomorrow?"

"Forever."

It was an unlikely way she'd met this man. An unlikely wife she'd made. But life with him was already better and fuller than her girlish dreams could ever have imagined.

Epilogue

Copper Creek, Colorado
1892

Kate squinted into the late afternoon sun and studied the approaching rider with butterflies of anticipation in her belly.

Noah.

He'd been gone a week, and she'd missed him so fiercely she could hardly sleep at night. But in this, their second year of marriage, she had finally learned that when he said he'd be back, he meant it. The occasional trips he took to buy stock were the only times they'd been apart. At first whenever he rode off she'd felt an oppressive sense of loss that she couldn't seem to shake.

But he always came back. Always.

He rode in close to the house where she stood on the bottom step of the porch, and eased from the saddle with a creak of leather and a fluid grace that still made her mouth go dry.

He lifted the weathered black hat from his head and hung it on the pommel before approaching. He hadn't shaved for a day or so, and his skin was burned from days in the sun, but he looked wonderful to her.

"I missed you somethin' fierce, Katherine Cutter."

Her heart did a backward stumble in her chest at his familiar voice and the words that spoke to her need. She brought a hand to her breast. "And I missed you."

She stood in his massive shadow now, squinting upward. "We need to talk," she told him.

His expression darkened. "Something wrong with Rose?"

"Rose is fine. Perfect." He'd seen to that, providing for them both and being a father to this child, just as he'd promised. "See? She's napping." She indicated the tiny form on the bunk which still had a place on the porch during warm months.

Noah took her hand and she led him to where

the toddler lay peacefully sleeping. Noah knelt at the side of the bed and ran his sunburned fingers over her pale blond hair in a gentle caress.

"You see, she's perfectly safe and healthy. Worn out from a morning of getting into everything."

"Did she miss me, too?"

"She asked about her papa every night."

He smiled and looked up at her. "Then what is it you have to talk to me about that makes you look so serious?"

"I was planning to wait and tell you tonight after you'd had a bath and a meal and a chance to rest."

He frowned. "Tell me what?"

She smoothed her palms over her skirt.

"Some might have said I was crazy for coming here with a man I'd never met before. For listening to his rash promise of a home and setting out without a backward glance. But I've never been so glad for anything, Noah."

He stood to his full height and studied her, his brown eyes filled with curiosity and love. "I'm the one who's thankful."

He took her hand and raised it to his lips.

She never noticed the scars any more, had

never cared much at all, actually. She reached up and cupped his beloved face in her palm.

His eyes darkened, but not with shame the way they once had, for now he believed in her love.

"What is it you have to tell me, then, Katy?"

She loved it when he called her Katy. She loved everything about the man. Anticipation made her throat tight. "There's going to be another member of the Cutter family."

He glanced at Rose and back. Realization dawned on his face in that split second.

"This Cutter will probably have darker hair and maybe brown eyes." She couldn't hold back the smile that sprang from her soul to express her supreme joy.

"Katy," he whispered. "A baby?"

She nodded through tears of happiness.

He gathered her to his chest so quickly and so closely, she could barely breathe. He smelled like sun and man and horse and his strong arms felt like heaven around her.

Once her dreams and her future had been dashed, but the love and caring of this man had restored her hope for fulfillment and happiness and had made all her wishes all come true.

Kate never regretted marrying Levi. If she hadn't, she'd never have had Rose, would never have met Noah.

Her heart was so full she couldn't imagine how it could possibly hold more love, but she knew that it would. She had a lot more love to give.

* * * * *

Discover Pure Reading Pleasure with

Visit the Mills & Boon website for all the latest in romance

 Buy all the latest releases, backlist and eBooks

 Find out more about our authors and their books

 Join our community and chat to authors and other readers

 Free online reads from your favourite authors

 Win with our fantastic online competitions

 Sign up for our free monthly eNewsletter

 Tell us what you think by signing up to our reader panel

 Rate and review books with our star system

www.millsandboon.co.uk

 Follow us at twitter.com/millsandboonuk

 Become a fan at facebook.com/romancehq